Universal Bureau of Copyrights

Universal Bureau of Copyrights

Bertrand Laverdure

Translated by Oana Avasilichioaei

BookThug · 2014

The production of this book was made possible through the generous assistance of
the Canada Council for the Arts and the Ontario Arts Council.

We acknowledge the financial support of the Government of Canada through the
National Translation Program for Book Publishing for our translation activities.

Canada Council　　**Conseil des Arts**
for the Arts　　　　**du Canada**

ONTARIO ARTS COUNCIL
CONSEIL DES ARTS DE L'ONTARIO
an Ontario government agency
un organisme du gouvernement de l'Ontario

LIBRARY AND ARCHIVES CANADA CATALOGUING IN PUBLICATION

Laverdure, Bertrand, 1967-
[Bureau universel des copyrights. English]
　　　Universal bureau of copyrights / Bertrand Laverdure ; translated by Oana
Avasilichioaei. – First English edition.

Translation of: Bureau universel des copyrights.
Issued in print and electronic formats.
ISBN 978-1-77166-052-5 (PBK.).–ISBN 978-1-77166-064-8 (HTML)

　　　I. Avasilichioaei, Oana, translator II. Title. III. Title: Bureau universel
des copyrights. English.

PS8573.A815B8713 2014　　　　C843'.54　　　C2014-904784-3
　　　　　　　　　　　　　　　　　　　　　　　　　C2014-904785-1

PRINTED IN CANADA

Freedom is a mystery.

— HELVETIUS

How could others, by their very nature, wish me well? At best, I trust in their curiosity and, more often than not, their predatory voracity. Desire is the others' infringement on me: violence and hope for happier shores, from which I could consider the other and myself as deadman anchors.

— RICHARD MILLET

1

At the Cirio in Brussels.

I just woke up.

Slept for about thirty minutes. That's all. Yet my entire life passed before my eyes like it does for the dying in an operetta. Only now, I had the feeling of really waking up, as if for the first time ever.

Everyone learns this at some point or other. Nature has no secret plan. Nature is not a kind organizer. Nature doesn't give a shit. She does her thing. Drops us through the hole, then waits.

Problem is, we all have illusions. We'd all love a purpose. Love to have our roles all set out, envision a grand plan, imagine that context, time, technology give us the benefit of distinction or even education, give us our blue blood, our late-night trysts, our heritage. All bullshit. Infantile drivel. There are never any options. We fall in and that's all.

As soon as we step outside we speed up the process. Think before you step.

Everything around me has taken on this tinge. Even the Italian waiter with his aggressive look and biting tongue seems more real.

We often live twofold, in our heads, then in our bodies. It's normal, natural; nature is complicated. Yet in waking I had the strange sensation that I live here and now, without a second of time difference. At last, at the focal point of a typically blurry objective. I don't ask myself who watches through the viewfinder though I know that most often we are outside the frame or absent. Then suddenly, I'm there and fall in step with the present's speed.

Event: the swinging door of the local jams up. One of the waiters goes to rescue the stuck customer. From afar I can't make it out well, but a large blue and white splotch greets the owner. I forget about my Rodenbach. A few customers begin to fuss over this fanatic in disguise. Several raise their glass as he passes. Sharp, pseudo-jackass eyes, corruption in his wake, this is a strange regular, I tell myself. I'm not dreaming either; this thing comes towards me. I refuse, at first, to identify him.

But resign myself to look at him. It's Jokey Smurf.

I use this major diversion to leave aside the impolite Italian waiter whom I'd love to knock out. Jokey Smurf deserves my full attention.

The Smurf hands me a present. The box we all know: yellow with a red ribbon. I feel like striking up a conversation with him.

He explains that he's never known what makes the box explode, but he's never had any doubt that it will explode. This Smurf is a notorious tautologist. In truth, he sees no further than his nostrils and this bugs me.

Me and Jokey Smurf, it just doesn't add up.

Since his conversation leads nowhere, a repetitive loop of two or three lax commonplaces, I quickly become supremely bored.

He seems disappointed by my irrepressible yawns. Between two takes of the same sample text monotonously recorded by a sullen actor, he re-hands me his present. I'm struck dumb.

Oscar Wilde predicted it: the only way to resist temptation is to succumb to it. There, it's done. I accept the present.

Naturally, the present explodes. Jokey Smurf bursts out laughing, as he should. Then, all of a sudden, I'm no longer there.

2

I reappear.

Blink my eyes two or three times to realize that my clandestine passenger body is resting on the cloth of a comfortable hammock. A bed of fortune held up by two solid straps, each wrapped around a trunk. I'm balancing between two trees with ludicrous nonchalance. Sausage of feet and legs, thorax and head, gently bound in its canvas skin.

I rest, relieved by my situation.

A few seconds is all it takes to realize the origin of the leafage around me and, incidentally, identify the source of various noises—the tennis balls and cars, the slight mayhem of picnics and baseball games: La Fontaine Park, southeast side, close to Sherbrooke Street.

I'm in Montreal, Quebec, surrounded by buildings, Notre-

Dame Hospital, a statue in honour of Charles de Gaulle—a genuine blue knife of cement piercing the clouds or an immense sundial, it depends.

From a leafy fold, the shadowy corner of a branch, I glimpse a squirrel, head lowered, suddenly advance. In a fury. A formidable fury. Piercing, magnetic sounds—like a badly playing track in a CD player or digitally treated noise—escape its snout. Annoyed by this unbearable monologue, I untangle myself from the hammock.

Then I walk away, heart in my throat.

The city abounds with numerous excessively subtle melodies, teeming sound curves. I'm all ears. Like Ulysses, let myself be carried away by the merchant murmur, the dense drone of the neighbourhood.

My new outlook and the ambient odours intermingle to form an ethereal mosaic. I feel protected. Walk leisurely along, like a great holy man or a stork.

We get used to everything. First to Mondays, then Tuesdays, then the rest of the week, the need to sleep, to amuse ourselves, then death. There is no universal truth, but cultivating our own truth helps pass the time. Mine doesn't correspond to yours but makes up for all the rest.

— Press play...

The squirrel panics. Hops up to me and grips onto my leg. More aggressive than a wolverine, its downy body a small docile bomb, it clutches at my skin with solid harness-claws. Its cutting teeth, a makeshift blade with anaesthetizing powers, begin to gnaw at the epidermis, dermis, then the muscles, the bone. My leg detaches, a flower unfolding.

I fall into a dark coma.

3

Crippled, I need to figure out how to fix my deficient loco-
motion. End up ripping off the pant leg, so that the loose
threads (skin and fabric) won't hinder my movements.

Suddenly, a crowd gathers. They bemoan my unlucky lot,
call the paramedics, take their time to faint, write sad verses,
speculate on the causes of my predicament. Upset by my
condition, an amateur musician stops noodling on his guitar,
abandons it under a tree in the park, then helps me to stand
and, declaring that he'll fix my problem, offers me the comfort of his car. Wearing a plethora of charms and trinkets, he
seems versed in the occult sciences. Naively, I ask him about
it. He replies that, to be more precise, he's a "collector." Out
of necessity rather than caution, I take my chances. Our mo-
bile journey puts my mind at ease. An amusing and talkative
polyglot (with even a basic understanding of Aramaic), this
Jonathan Bélanger makes conversation while I attempt to
get my new posterior as comfortable as optimally possible

on the seat of his car.

A curious collector, he tells me he owns a good hundred artificial legs, made in different eras. He's a connoisseur of orthopaedic devices and an enthusiast of African art.

He makes me wait a long time in front of his house. The neighbourhood is shady, the alleys are garbage-strewn. Five scruffy kids loiter on the street corner, a toothless old man in an Expos baseball cap sips his afternoon beer. A quiet, desolate place. Scratching my thigh brings some relief.

The collector returns with a retractable wheelchair, an old model.

Somehow or other, I manage to slide into the chair. He pushes me to the door.

In his basement, which I reach by clutching onto his sleeves and straining my abdominal muscles a few times, he parks the wheeled contraption in a corner. All around the walls hang artificial limbs, canes, primitive flutes, Dogon ornaments and statuettes from Sudan, Mali, Ethiopia, Burkina Faso, hollow sticks, oblong faces excessively stretched out, giant amulets for elephants, cylindrical masques and other wooden art objects. He hesitates for a moment. Slowly closes his eyes. Reopens them with great calm, then walks towards a giant teak chest with a frieze portraying a traditional antelope hunting scene of spears, the cornering of the prey and the dismembering of the animal. Once opened, the great trunk releases an odour of fresh tobacco and cigars. He rummages inside for some time. Hard wooden pieces bang against each other. Gently, he pulls out a jointed sculpture of some indefinite material and hands me the object.

Examining it closely, I realize it's an ornamental wooden leg, particularly well-crafted, with an impressive knee reflex action mechanism. Carved out of some sort of jet-black wood, this work of art could have figured in any cabinet of curiosities.

Overcome once more with a spiritual presence, and apropos of my new acquaintance, I suddenly envision a devout gesture and slowly raise the wooden leg above my head. In my own way, I pay tribute to the human capacity for invention, which unexpectedly moves me. As impassive and mute now as he had been chatty and mischievous earlier, Jonathan Bélanger breathes without a sound, then rubs his slightly irritated right eye.

Politely, he takes the object from my hands and fingers it cautiously. He seems to be assessing its strength, looking for defects that could remove the object's magical charm. After a few moments of sombre silence, a generous smile lights up his face.

"Encore," he says to me.

Not quite knowing what to say to this truncated phrase, I simply nod my head. He continues, laboriously, to explain. In four attempts at elocution he manages to formulate a robotic phrase: "Encore is the name."

He repeats this phrase several times. "Encore is the name. Encore is the name."

In a wheelchair, in a cluttered basement, I feel confined. Start losing my patience. Nervous, I begin manhandling the shoulder of my unhinged interlocutor. Suspicious of all this repetitive benevolence and motivated by a desire to promptly take care of the stagnation, I deal him a dizzying blow to the stomach, then topple to the floor. He bends over in pain, choking, and in the confusion crashes against a pair of black jointless legs, wrenching them off the wall in his fall.

Both of us are now in truce mode. Externally, I hold back. Yet I'm boiling with the fury of a frightened one-legged man who feels that a trap could close in on him at any moment. I grab at his sweater, shake him à la Lino Ventura. Then aptly ask, "What are you talking about?"

The collector's jaw swells with every passing minute, his cheek muscles gradually get rigid, I melt with rage. Yet before I have the nerve to pummel his face, three other words escape his gullet: "The leg's name."

He falls asleep immediately.

I give up. This type of object is its own legend. I extract the jointed wooden piece from the soft grip of my saviour. Take it upon myself to give it a noble purpose, a matter of not causing too much remorse.

I match the tip of the wooden piece to the stump of my thigh. I want to win the leg over, take up residence in it. An artwork that will transform me into an artwork: art contaminates everything it touches.

Encore fits me like a glove. I try to not be surprised.

Liberated from my momentary torpor and struck with unusual life force, I lean on the wall to reach a standing position. Manage to haul up my carcass by alternately dragging my dead leg and living leg. Putting some shoulder force into it, I take up my bipedal appearance.

Plant my feet flat on the ground. I'm finally standing upright.

Right then the collector tries to wake up. But when he opens his eyes, they emit a thick smoke. From all the orifices of his head, a black gas emanates. His face is now a fire pit. Then his body is consumed. The fire takes over the entire room in record time. In this basement trap, nothing is visible anymore.

4

My foot made a knock.

The twenty-or-so people standing around take no notice of my appearance. Inveterate aficionados of libertarian idleness, the customers continue to sip their drinks. If you removed the glasses from all the people sitting alone in all the world's bars, you'd end up with the image of an underwater cemetery.

My left hand grips the banister of the spiral staircase cut in a flowing aluminium. I go up. Encore executes the task assigned to it with panache. This reassures me. The sophisticated furnishings of the room on the second floor are in harmony with the rest of the place.

Curious, I go back to the pub's entrance, where I discover a metal display case with numerous small compartments. It's basically a stand of brochures, leaflets, flyers and advertising postcards. Vivid colours clash. Matte and glossy finishes fight for attention. In the pile, I notice a pink card, a *très* dandy photo of Serge Gainsbourg and Jane Birkin: Gainsbourg in a pinstripe suite and Birkin in miniskirt and schoolgirl stockings. The muse of *L'Homme à tête de chou*,[1] her left leg raised at a right angle, is glued to her lover's body as if preparing to mount him, while he stands impassive with his right hand on her bare hip. Using Photoshop, an outstretched black wing, *très* BD, got added to Gainsbourg's back. In a pink bubble by Birkin's knee are three grainy, bloated, cursive letters, RDB, which seem to have been photocopied twice before ending up on the card.

I go outside to look at the building's exterior. Sheer curiosity. High up, above the corner entrance of the establishment, I read: Le Roi des Belges.[2] From which, undoubtedly, the three letters, RDB.

On the back of the pink card, I read the same words, then above, in very refined handwriting, the name of the bar on the second floor, the Royal Cocktail Bar. I walk with my prosthetic leg without feeling any change in my gait. I've mastered the technique of the pendulum. One of my feet will always make a "knock." I'm getting used to this new minimalist percussive tool.

---

1. *L'Homme à tête de chou (The Man with the Cabbage Head)* is a concept album by Serge Gainsbourg issued in 1976. (trans.)
2. *The King of the Belgians* (trans.)

Trustful out of necessity, I make my way back to the stairs and return to the second-floor lounge. Of average capacity, seating no more than twenty asses, the bar, streaked in the half-light of the still-open daytime blinds, exudes a nonexistent ambiance. The stools, shaped like truncated cones, stuffed and upholstered in red velvet, inspire comfort.

I take over a table hidden in a corner next to the stairs. My eyes gradually adjust to the sombre lighting in the room and it's only once I've acclimatized myself to the weak glare that I make out the presence of two customers.

At the bar, I recognize the charming blue mascot. In off-mode, serene in his role as exploiter. His two arms rest on the counter, one extended, the other bent at the elbow, well-fastened to a glass of Maes. The beer glass is empty, but the Smurf refuses, for some unknown reason, to set it down. At his feet, his tool: the yellow box with a large red ribbon.

Near the stage—a simple plywood platform painted black—a young woman fiddles with her Bloody Mary, captivated by the clinking ice cubes. In the background, "Sunday Morning" by the Velvet Underground plays. The few bars of the glockenspiel that begin the tune resist the dim light. Then Lou Reed's voice fills the room with an easygoing calm from another era.

The young woman catches my eye, leaves off playing with her drink. With striking nonchalance she takes a swig of her beverage, then sets down the green plastic stirring stick shaped like a stylized crocodile. Her upper lip still moist with tomato juice, she patiently opens her mouth and calls out to me.

Jokey Smurf stretches out his elbow, then sinks back into apathy.

Some twenty seconds pass. We remain alone in this deserted lounge in the middle of the afternoon. Offended by my lack of initiative, the young woman grabs the green stick and flings it at my face. The projectile strikes my nose. She laughs wholeheartedly. Which makes me bite back the two invectives that would have landed on deaf ears. All childishness.

Anyone who teases you gently, without malice, has some tenderness for you. Don't chase them away, above all don't camouflage yourself in rage: banish your bitterness and get in tune. So I go for a laugh. With my right index finger, I tap my nose, then mime a huge pulsing swelling. I inflate my jowls, imitating a squirrel. I am a sad clown. I roll my eyes, then smash my head on the small table. Rather à la Chaplin.

My little burlesque number won her smile. She came over to

join me.

We talked for at least two hours. The conversation's topics proliferated, we kept finding a pretext to relaunch. A harmonious cocoon lasting only for the duration of our first encounter. We covered many easy subjects, like the Velvet Underground's album covers, Andy Warhol's dissolute life and Basquiat's haircuts. But when I quickly passed over the tragic death of Nico, singer and muse of Reed and Warhol, she glared at me, insanely pissed off. A crazy thought had jammed a gear in her brain.

She began talking only of Nico, throwing a fit, getting agitated, losing her reasoning faculties. Nico's appearance in Fellini's *La Dolce Vita*, her unlucky love for Lenny Bruce, her German past during the war, the collaboration with the Velvet Underground, the end of her life, destitute, confined to her barrel organ, playing old hits, then her ridiculous death while biking in Ibiza. My counterpart was animated with an inexplicable rage.

Annoyed, I seized her hands, which were bopping in the air to the tempo of her intemperance, and repeatedly told her that an artist's fate is sometimes cruel, that fame will never be worth a hundred good conversations with true friends, and that her death no longer makes anyone cry.

She looked at me abruptly, stiff with terror. I immediately apologized, understanding that I'd crossed the line of her dignity.

Out of the blue, the Smurf stirred from his stupor. He came towards us, held out his playful package to my interlocutor.

Contrary to what the comic protocol imposes on the confection of an explosive present, this one, oddly enough, had an empty side, the opposite of which had two average-size holes, large enough to engulf two hands.

Considerate, the Smurf nodded his head and looked at Nico's groupie. He oddly prompted her to manoeuvre the empty box in a novel ritual.

After a few seconds of juggling the object, the woman, sniggering, finally found a use for the thing and hid her breasts by stuffing them into the open side of the box. I was taken aback.

"Do you know the artist Valie Export?" she asked.

I told her no. She then launched into a short explanatory monologue, entirely theatrical, full of grandiloquent pauses. She gave me a broad outline of the Austrian artist's life: Waltraud Lehner, better known as Valie Export, was made famous in 1968 for her legendary performance *Tapp und Tastkino/Tap and Touch Cinema*. The performance consisted of her wearing a cardboard box on her bare chest, the box fitted with two ventral openings. Her very own little theatre if you like. The performance's male visitors were invited to stick their hands into the box and touch her breasts. A gesture that became erotic, intimate and controversial all at once.

Her exposé completed, she gave me a big smile. A Cheshire cat or Stepford wife kind of smile.

The Smurf, who, prudently, had stepped back from the woman's emotional sphere of influence, was chuckling behind his cartoonish hand.

Transfixed by her radiant smile, I lost track of my hands. Undisciplined and predatory, these very hands slipped into the box to cop a feel of the offered breasts.

Jokey started to get bored. Announced that he would take back the present, that all this had stopped being funny.

Clearly, the pleasure of others got on his nerves.

When I managed to take control of my hands, they'd

changed. Completely missing the little fingers, they now had only four digits.

My hands had mutated.

5

Disturbing vibrations in my ear canal. My head and back are black and blue. I open my eyes. My ear is resting on a bed of rocks, scalp pressed to a rail track.

My body resembles a Nordic vessel that's run aground. A few idle onlookers barely disguise their surprise. Nobody wants to offend anyone. It's impolite. Suddenly, a feminine hand grabs my own. Startled, I get up. The tram arrives at the station five seconds later. I stare at my saviour.

— Who are you?

— My name is Françoise. You almost stayed there for good.

The good Samaritan doesn't want to release her hold. She continues to clench my hand. I politely shake off her forearm. She points out that I only have four digits left. The tram leaves the station. A drawn-out noise of scraping metal floods the terminal, which is an immense cavern plastered throughout with white and blue tiles, several bearing letters.

I turn to read the station's name, Sint-Gillis Voorplein, written in Flemish on the tunnel vault.

When my gaze meets the woman's eyes once more, she hands me a scrap of paper. It's her turn, she seems to be insinuating, to ask something of me. Yet as soon as I grab hold of the paper, she starts walking away. I don't understand her hurry.

— But where are you off to?

— I'm leaving.

Alone on the platform, feeling agitated, I take the time to sit on one of the discoloured seats intended for commuters. A rest is necessary.

I examine the paper. Before me is a long text printed recto-verso. It's a copy of a webpage listing all the articles of the Universal Declaration of Human Rights, adopted by the members of the United Nations in 1948.

The mysterious wise woman has taken the time to highlight in a greenish-yellow Article 26 of the Declaration:

1. Everyone has the right to education. Education shall be free, at least in the elementary and fundamental stages. Elementary education shall be compulsory. Technical and professional education shall be made generally available and higher education shall be equally accessible to all on the basis of merit.

2. Education shall be directed to the full development of the human personality and to the strengthening of respect for human rights and fundamental freedoms. It shall promote understanding, tolerance and friendship among all nations, racial or religious groups, and shall further the activities of the United Nations for the maintenance of peace.

3. Parents have a prior right to choose the kind of education that shall be given to their children.

Glancing back and forth several times between the sheet of paper and the station's tiles, I realize that this famous Article 26 is in fact the text running along the terminal's walls. I'm stunned.

I wander through the innards of the Universal Declaration of Human Rights. A strong humanist feeling awakens all my pores, gives me goosebumps. Shouldn't have stood up so quickly from my seat. I wait for the feeling to fade.

The aforementioned Françoise is already far off. I spot her at the end of the passageway leading to Place Saint-Gilles. I get going again, thinking to go catch up with the messenger. At first I run slowly, then pick up the pace.

In leaving, I notice Jokey Smurf. First, a blue halo, then the outline of his body, his voice, then the sound of his soft booties on the tram platform. I keep running.

He says abruptly:

— They're going to flood the tunnel!

I ask:

— Who are "they"?

For an answer, he slaps me on the back, pushing me towards the exit.

Suddenly I hear Françoise who, by a stroke of bad luck, has returned to her starting point along the rail tracks. She screams, water licks at her calves, an immense whirlpool engulfs the underground passage; from where I'm standing I can smell the foul odour of the sewer water invading the place.

The Smurf and I come out onto Place Saint-Gilles, in front of the church.

Only now do we realize the fury of the flood.

A geyser of water bursts outside through the revolving door, swallowing up the stalls of the carpet, tablecloth and fabric sellers.

I take shelter in front of the church, under the bas-relief of Saint Gilles protecting a doe, who has itself sought refuge in the hermit's cave.

I recall that he can be invoked against madness.

This crosses my mind when I raise my eyes to admire the craftsmanship of the pediment.

I hear the fire truck sirens. The Smurf has disappeared. Françoise is undoubtedly drowning at this very moment.

The church door opens. Someone makes a sign for me to enter.

6

An old man slaps my face.

I'm slumped over like a vagrant, head flat on a paper place-mat that lists the menu, the scrap of cellulose sticking to my cheek.

At the back of the room, beneath a large decorative shark with its jaw agape, a bearded man in his thirties is talking into a megaphone.

He directs the sound of his voice at the washroom wall, which is a large bevelled mirror. Each corner is decorated with what I'd vaguely describe as a "western" pattern.

This is what he says:

— Customer collapsed on a table. Snoring. An old man de-cides to administer a whack to wake him up.

The old man greets me with a comical bow. I pull myself together and thank him.

— The old man is on the case, but keeps his distance. The other man, disconcerted, seems to be looking in my direction. Will there be some verbal exchange between these two individuals or not?

The heckler on the megaphone reports all my movements, comments on my body's reactions, then moves on to other customers in the restaurant. His bearing resembles that of a commentator thrust into an experience with no way out, having to describe the movements of reality as reflected in the washroom mirror of this twenty-four-hour diner.

In the kitchen, one or two individuals give orders. I notice too the substantial quantity of dishes waiting on the serving counter.

A very pretty young woman in a sky-blue jacket and yellow tights hands me a small card with a smiling guy on the front and hand diagrams explaining words in sign language on the back. A waitress arrives at the same time.

The crier on the megaphone continues his commentary:

— A waitress approaches the individual. The man hesitates. Seems confused...

I stop listening to the crank's report when I feel my prosthesis move. My wooden leg creaks, lets out a unique whistle that I find slightly irritating. My crafted leg appears to be talking. Though to be more precise, it would be truer to say that she is whistling or wheezing, more like a mechanical bird than an organic creature. I lean over, prick up my ears. A gentle, sinusoidal lament escapes from my ligneous appendage. Somewhat electronic, like the sound a theremin makes.

Suddenly the restaurant is plunged into a morbid silence.

Encore fills the void. Penetrates everyone's ears, takes control of bodies. Megaphone man falls quiet as well. Even takes the opportunity to move closer to my table, like a lemur or some other strange animal.

I am spellbound by the sounds of my leg. Silence continues to swoop down wherever the natural sounds of mouths, conversations, frying or cooking had previously reigned. Encore expresses herself despite my astonishment, lets escape a phenomenal amount of varied and shrill sounds through all the cracks and holes adorning her wooden dress.

The sermonizing bullhorn sits down on the banquette opposite me. He's now at my table. With ceremonial slowness, he swings his megaphone around so that the end that amplifies the voice is now close to my singing leg. In short, he decides to pass the mic to Encore.

I accept that my wooden leg sings. Soon, the megaphone will inundate this good old restaurant called Miami with a particularly melancholic lament composed for solo leg.

Once mirror-man has finished adjusting the mic, the whole restaurant resonates with the song of absent leg. A moment of grace, I'd say, a moment of grandiose devotion.

Fiuuuuuuuuuuuuuuuuouiiiiiiiiiiiiiiiiiiiiiiiiiiitiouuuuuuuuuuuu uuuueiyaouuuuuuuuuuuuuuuuufiuuuuuuuuuuuuuoiaoiaaaaoi aaaoiaaaaaaaaaaaaaaaaaaaaaaaaaxyuuuuuuyuuuuuuuu

Clumsily, I try to jot down the sounds erupting from my prosthesis, but without success.

Transfixed, everyone is courageously listening to the concert. No one dares say anything; some drool over their plates, others slowly withdraw a forkful from their sated mouths. It's obvious that the room wants an explanation for what is happening. The strange commentator undoubtedly would have forged some pleasing description of the events. Yet his state of concentration is such that you'd think he's been bewitched. Basically, any commentator, even one who preaches the harsh reality of sports at ungodly hours, would be welcomed with a satisfied smile by those present. The first man to name things is always the one who calms the flock.

Suddenly I feel air escaping from the commentator's ear. A thick jet.

With astonishing speed, megaphone man deflates, just like a beach ball. His legs lose their volume, his head sags on the table, his shoulders settle on the banquette, dragging along in their fall the pelvis, buttocks and most of the back. As soon as this destabilizing effect reaches his right hand, the megaphone, lacking support, and freed from the hand's grasp, crashes on into the varnished floor. It goes without saying that Encore's song is accordingly cut short. Deprived of her worthy amplifier, the unsteady melody of the stiff leg resumes its reedy murmur. All those initially dumbfounded slowly start to lose their composure. The situation frightens some of the customers, who begin to make their way towards the exit, leaving a rough amount for their order (eaten or not) under saltshaker, cutlery, or in disorder in the middle of the table, the bills crumpled, folded into strips or paper airplanes—flimsy tokens of conventional courtesy—before marching in military step towards the vestibule.

The aquariums near the entrance burst, injuring some of the fugitives.

From the kitchen, a surge of seawater rushes out and engulfs the entire place in just a few minutes. Trimmings, plastic flowers, stuffed parrots and fish come unhooked from the walls.

I confess to getting stopped at the entrance by flying glass, which rips part of my right arm. Tendons, bones and muscles in the salt. Water seeps into my wound cauterizing it. At first, I feel nothing but a brutal emotional shock. Though sharp pain soon finds its way.

Describing the chaos that takes over everything as of this moment would be in vain. "Jumping into a mess" or "jumping into the fray" are expressions that only provide us with a choice of poor nuances. Using the word "hell" would be too extreme or insidiously picturesque.

One of the victims decided to break the picture window that overlooks the terrace in front of the restaurant. In the frantic flooding, I don't have time to delight in this breach.

All at once, a plastic swordfish comes unhooked from the chains fastening it to the ceiling, bounces on the water one second before making a nosedive, grazing the head of a petrified old woman, its spear still unsullied by live flesh, to finish its drop in the remains of my right forearm, thus completely detaching it from my body.

7

Where does the category of "character" end? Where does the category of "truth" begin?

A man with an amputated right arm floats in the basin of the fountain in Place d'Espagne, Brussels, close to the Galeries Saint-Hubert. With his stump sticking out of the water and his face half-submerged, he is having trouble breathing.

All this time, no passerby has thought it wise to save this man who's obviously in bad shape. Besides, why save a character? It's pointless. For several minutes, the patched-up character continues to survive despite appearances. The strangest aspect of the whole thing is that no onlooker has gotten it wrong: he is, in fact, a character. So all bets are off.

Except a nice Russian couple, musicians. The man plays a handmade double bass, fashioned out of a long string attached to the centre of a metal basin and held taut with a broomstick, while his green-skirted companion applies herself to an accordion.

Coming out of the Galeries Saint-Hubert, Jokey Smurf passes them. Motivated by the prospect of catching more prey, he holds out an entirely new present to the bass player. The street artist, guileless, friendly and pleased by the gift, nods, accepts and starts to open the surprise. The Smurf steps back, as can be expected. A tremendous flash followed by a long plume of white and blue smoke envelopes the wretch who, considering the violence of the shock, is grimacing and hardly laughing. His companion reacts at once. She pitches her accordion at the Smurf's head, still within reach. Misunderstanding hovers. The blue character falls unconscious on the cobblestones. Smoke-man continues to bat at the air around him. He paddles with his arms, as if he's trying to get out of an asphyxiating tunnel in a serious fire. When he realizes that only one of his arms is responding, he almost panics, but then he too prefers to lose consciousness. Another one-armed man is added to our story. What's more, he too has lost his right arm.

It's at this point that a troop of literary tourists intervenes. For the first time, all the members of the gang, who haven't necessarily read the book but who have followed, with guide and road maps, our hero's adventures, show up on the scene.

The guide suggests to his group to go assess the state of the main character in the fountain. A moustached rebel, who has paid for his "tourist for a few chapters" pass like all the other members of the package tour, reacts to this decision, effectively stealing the floor from the guide.

— I'm sure that the main character's stump should have grown back. It's not in the brochure, but you can bet your ass there's been some negligence in the writing of this scene.

Arriving at the fountain and leaning over the main character's body, moustache-man apprehends that the former is still alive, but getting weaker by the minute. His illusions are shattered. He touches the healthy arm lying in the water and the bloody stump, which is in a bad state and continues to taunt him. There is no new right arm just like there is no permutation of arms. Everything is in place in the best of all worlds.

— Two right arm stumps, it's very disappointing. I want my money back.

The other tourists remind him that the information given was undoubtedly sound and that, anyway, soon they will all receive a new edition of this famous map of future narrative events. Everyone is hungry. The guide takes the opportunity to announce a free hour. The malcontent invites his comrades to the first waffle stand they can find. He wants to apologize by treating everyone to waffles. A lout, but generous all the same. Apart from two people, one frustrated, the other resting, the rest of the group is salivating in anticipation of the crunchy-soft goodness of this tasty concoction. Very few people take action, and that's where the drama lies, but also the comedy.

*

In the main character's skull, there is also action.

(In the background can be heard the constant sound of water weakly lapping in the fountain.)

So... honestly, why am I sulking in gloom when I should be extricating myself from the fountain (mouth noises) my legs are out cold... my working arm prefers to float (violent mouth noises) it's not going well... yeah, yeah, I'm hanging on... we can't get rid of this natural passage... good old holes that press us and test us... and... what... I could've died squashed by an elephant, crushed in a garbage truck, suffocated by a pretzel, poisoned by a bay leaf, struck down by a heart attack in a bus at rush hour... this doesn't make me feel better ... not at all... got to be consistent... we plasticize, download, digitize, modernize, we clean better, heal faster, we do everything faster, but no one has figured out how to patch up the hole of the living... the vast infinite hole into which we all fall... I mean the hole that, joined end to end with others' holes since the beginning of time, forms an infinite tunnel, a dark labyrinth, from which we all spring up, wherever we can, wherever there's copulation, in other words everywhere, and then... but what is... what is this (prolonged mouth noises)... what do they have to laugh about, these dandified flâneurs... I wonder... my nose tells me I'm alive... I struggle for my nose... brave slender bellhops in front of the flooded hotel... they look me over... an agitated moustached guy leans over me... the little shit is worried... these idiots are always worried... they don't wait... they want us immediately within their reach... they spring up out of nowhere to gut us with whatever shovel is on hand... as soon as it suits their next idiocy... I feel sorry for him... he looked thoroughly disappointed... thoroughly... but who's going to get me out of here... once and for all... really (mouth noises) I feel some tingling in my legs... my arms... it's coming back... one small step... one small dry step.

8

Those less inclined to understand are always the most in a hurry to act.

In short, bored with the lack of events happening in their news box, the troop of literary tourists returned to the crime scene. An elderly literary tourist, kinder than the others, disapproved of leaving a character, even if only a paper animal, to face a symbolic certain death in a public fountain.

With aplomb that spurred his pupils into action (his job compels him to develop a kind of educational tenderness for his tourists), the guide took charge of the general manoeuvres. Promptly, he chose four beefy guys, including the moustached hothead, to go find a stretcher at the Factory of Realistic Objects office. They returned successful from their expedition. The four scoundrels were now ready to carry out their mission: extract the main character from the fountain in Place d'Espagne.

Which was accomplished in no time. They laid him on the ground, then gave him new clothes.

*

All my limbs are reacting to my nerves. I'm feeling much better. I'm dry. I'm well. Took the time to thank the empathetic crowd around me. I notice the fool with the moustache who seems to have chosen a much more deserving position by keeping back from the action.

In front of the Galeries Saint-Hubert (I suddenly recognize the place), the Smurf, squatting down, rubs his head, then redons his white hat while an ambulance gobbles up the musician who refuses to let go of his strange double bass until a paramedic tears it out of his hand, and who, incidentally, is also missing his right arm. The coincidence upsets me, but what can I do about it? His companion, in tears, goes to sit beside him in the ambulance. She gives the Smurf an indignant look. He doesn't react. Once again, the Smurf has made someone the butt of a joke; of course, he's programmed for it, a knee-jerk reaction. What's more, the mechanics of his actions are so pitiful that people should start to watch out. But we persist, I don't really know why, in giving him more attention than he deserves. The police don't come, because the police never lift a finger to lock up a character. Characters have the good life, and I'm not complaining because I'm part of their ridiculous Aeropagus.

Through careful consideration, I have calmly learned how to become a character. It demands constant application. I wasn't a character at the beginning of this book, but I have become one.

I'm walking in circles, distracted, limping appropriately and content, a few screws loose in my head, always on a quest for an answer to all of this.

A man in his thirties, wearing a white chef's hat and a jacket with the word "Neuhaus" embroidered in cursive script, calls me over with his finger. I think he's inviting me to visit his shop. The reasons for his standing there are beyond me. He touches his right shoulder with his left index finger. He insists. I look at my stump. He nods his head. Then touches his right shoulder with his other hand for a second time. He's trying to tell me something in a language I don't really understand. I get closer, murmur in his ear that he can address me in French, but he continues his voiceless routine. I say, "OK," simply to produce something that could begin to resemble some kind of answer for him. These two letters have their effect; he takes my hand and pulls me unceremoniously into the back of his chocolate shop.

I am inside a maze of vats, plastic-covered trays and marble slabs.

He suddenly stops in front of a glass bell. I look at him, he looks at me, we look at each other. I shrug my shoulders. Venture to tell him "OK" again, instinctually knowing that this magical word can, in this case, protect us from all forms of narrative stagnation. I test it out. He stirs, pulls on a wooden tab that reveals an empty space under the glass bell. Using the most rudimentary crank, like a traditional hand brace, he activates a mechanism that slowly lifts a shining piece of metal, crafted by a skilled artisan, out of the hole. The object, resembling an average-sized arm, is divided in four parts that fit together with movable catches. It's a sort of metal shell fitted with a jointed hand. At first glance, it looks like a piece of armour. But on closer examination, it's a sophisticated culinary mould.

I see the exhaustion return to my host's eyes. Again feel fatigue in my jaws. Not a good sign; I'm stressed out. Then I regain my self-control. These utilitarian characters, these video game clowns don't deserve for us to dwell on them too much. So I decide to speed things up and see how far his programming has been set. I tell him in gaga tongue:

— OK, OK, OK, OK, OK, OK, OK, OK, OK.

I see him squirm like a fish chomping with foolish fervour on a wriggling worm. He bustles about, settles down, lifts the glass bell, grabs the metal arm, leaves the room for a few seconds, comes back, puts down the contraption with catches, makes two or three other moves that elude me, clasps my hand, pats my head, leaves again, comes back a few minutes later, jumps on the spot, dances a surprising Irish jig, then goes to sit on a varnished wooden chair in the corner of the room. Apparently, this android was fabricated to make people laugh. I can't help displaying an uneasy grimace. Naturally, he doesn't notice anything and it's just as well. Impassive, serene, he shows me a calendar that hangs just above him. His extremely agile left index finger taps the next day's date. He most certainly wants me to come back in twenty-four hours. A good interpreter of others' vacuities, I bow down. His programmed finger keeps rhythmically taping the relatively narrow box on the calendar. With the utmost precision, the tip of his nail touches the centre of the square. The obsessive repetition of this gesture makes a tiny notch, then gradually begins to pierce the page. Dismayed, I go to the trouble of uttering the fateful expression one last time: "OK." In a flash, his arm regains its position on his chest.

9

Twenty-four hours later, I stood in exactly the same spot where I had thought it wise the day before to fire the last practical "OK" that put an end to our initial meeting.

A scrupulous stage manager, who had made sure to mark an X with gum tape where my feet should stand, was surprised by the accuracy of my memory. I was bang on the spot. Twenty-four hours earlier, twenty-four hours later, nothing had moved, nothing had changed. Accordingly, I stood ready and waited with gaiety as much as with indifference.

It's well known that secondary characters don't make main characters wait, so a few seconds were all it took for the automaton in the chef's hat to reappear in my field of vision. It's useless here to recapitulate his getup, the initial program didn't plan a wardrobe for the gentleman. So, in the customary uniform, the master chocolatier of Neuhaus greets me with respect. A last-minute addition to his panoply of gestures, I can only imagine. He then begins to give an encore of touching his right shoulder with the left index finger, the now legendary choreography that bores me a little, though less than yesterday since I see in this gesture a commendable attempt at communication. I greet him back with the unusual "OK," pronouncing each letter exceedingly firmly. The comic affect can't be helped. I laugh silently. End of the break.

Momentarily, he disappears into the next room. A long time passes.

When he returns, he's holding an enormous rectangular gift box at arm's length. The box is wrapped, tied and adorned with a ribbon, and crowned by a pink and yellow rosette of indecent proportion.

Spontaneously, I say "Thank you," which causes no reaction in my interlocutor. I change my tactic. Looking for new challenges, I get the idea of writing the word "OK" on a sheet of paper and using it as bait. I've become mischievous. It takes longer than usual since I have to try to write the letters with my left hand. The result looks like a young child's scribble. After a few minutes of fooling around, weary, I pronounce a very loud, very round, very audible "OK."

In response to my new command, he makes one last, deep obeisance and hastily leaves the room.

I'm left alone.

No, there is also a box. A gift meant for me, it seems.

With only one arm to rip open the wrapping paper and unknot the ribbon, I used my teeth. It took some patience but the box gave way.

In the box, resting in a setting of blue silk, I discover a chocolate arm. Not an arm of milk chocolate, but rather a very dark, smooth arm of a chocolate so dense and polished that it reflects the light. At the elbow, wrist and finger joints, there is an ingenious mechanism made of marzipan balls and slender sticks of barley sugar.

At this juncture, the moustache-man from the literary tourist group gives me an outrageously comical pat on the left shoulder.

I turn around.

The entire gang of idiots, all the imbeciles from yesterday, are staring at me.

— My God, my God, what are you doing here? (This is what I finally say aloud.)

— My dear sir, we are here to watch. We paid our "walking-tour" fee. Our guide provided us with a map of the narrative on which are marked a few points of interest. The installing of your chocolate arm is an event rated four out of five stars.

I'm annoyed. But in view of the evidence, I must give in. This arm will become my second prosthesis. With or without the spectators, I would have come to the same conclusion. I affix the jointed appendage to my rosy stump.

I align the artwork to my shoulder. Who here wouldn't be surprised to find the chocolate, marzipan and barley sugar instantly metamorphose into veins, muscles, bones and skin? I now have a wooden, music-loving, musician-leg, an arm of hard chocolate, one less little finger, and a literary tourist group on my heels.

I suffer the impudent applause of the stupid group. Then kindly ask them to let me pass. I must leave.

10

Without looking back, with no Orpheus costume, no unseemly vengeance, I start walking beneath the arched glass roof of the Galeries Saint-Hubert—an aesthetic microcosm and herald of inelegant North-American shopping malls. Or rather a precursor. Commerce always evolves faster than the human form.

Strolling people cut me off, overtake me, walk around me. I am a moving milestone making its way through the city.

Besides, I am walking with a Wong Kar-Wai slowness. The mechanics of all my bones engage in slow motion; I see the ground coming, assess it, anticipate it, raise my eyes, make eye contact with others. I have a strong impression of contributing to the totality of a parallel world, stuck in my cubicle of witness-observer, apart from all the rest.

What I follow doesn't lead to anything except to my own person. I feel this truth profoundly.

Moreover, my steps follow a trajectory that will force me to pass through a newsstand extending out into the middle of the Saint-Hubert gallery. Keeping watch from revolving stands with gilt hinges, hundreds of daily and weekly newspapers from all over the world spread international news like weeds. Millions of lines report everyone's problems, political scandals, sports events, soporific financial news which, written in code for the initiated, sometimes transforms into famine, trade surplus, job loss, or the great mayhem of international indifference.

In fact, I cause an accident.

To tell the truth, I suddenly charge into one of the stands.

In short, I found myself with my face pressed into *L'Osservatore Romano*, chocolate arm squashed into a pile of *Die Zeit*, wooden leg stuck in the *New York Times*, and right hand torn through a special edition of the *Corriere della Sera*.

It wasn't long before a human voice materialized. The owner of the newsstand—a young Arab man—sprung up almost immediately from behind the cash register. He railed me with a pack of insults and starts miming a raging buffalo. Disturbing.

— Moron! Cantcha watch where ya put yer feet?

He has a sharp-looking mug and a lean jaw. Not at all the physiognomy of a bon vivant with weak principles. He is a vehicle for strong convictions, you can feel it. Besides, once he got down to my level and noticed my glaring handicaps, his young head began looking like that of a penitent cat. For a few seconds, his mouth hung open, his tongue idle.

— My brother! I'm so sorry. I'm the moron, the tight-ass, ya get me? I'll help ya, there, give me yer hand.

Rushing to get me back on my feet, he forgets to set upright the revolving stand, from which *L'Osservatore Romano* pontificates about the world. He invites me to the back of his shop for some mint tea.

I am captivated by the nature of his conversation, the kindness of his remarks, his consideration. He asks me the usual questions about the strange prostheses I sport. I took the time to recount some plausible stories that I won't repeat here.

He seemed to believe me, asked forgiveness again, full of compassion, overly obsequious, overly sensitive.

The name of this human being, properly educated in the script of predictable sympathy, is Sambal Oelek.

I only had a fraction of a second to notice a Smurf before getting hit in the head with a miserable projectile and losing consciousness.

Barely managed to address this mischance, the arbitrary power providing me with all these powerful sensations: "Hello, automaton."

11

I'm neither standing nor sitting, but rather leaning at an angle, head resting on a leather stool. Don't need to see the material to recognize it. A clingy membrane smelling of animal.

I straighten up. Lean on the small piece of furniture. All my senses have now adjusted to the weak light. What I see shocks me without being able to say why at first. It's beyond me; I feel embittered, consumed with a throbbing unease. Getting the distinct impression of having landed in a monstrous mental vortex.

What I see is an extremely long corridor, quite narrow and gleaming, of non-functional breadth, meant to run behind a stage, serve as an emergency exit or a secondary passageway.

Everywhere along one side of the corridor, at regular intervals of about three metres, hang Smurf costumes. Hundreds of Smurf costumes ironed and pinned to the wall with their four-digit gloves and stock of surprise boxes. These distinctive threads would easily attire an entire battalion of the detestable beings.

I take a moment. Sit down on the stool, legs far apart, like a farmer yoked to a plough. No sound comes to disturb the steady progress of my stupefaction.

Where exactly am I? Behind the scenes of the book?

Silence drops its storm sail.

Then, adrenaline surges in me like a bionic plant, releases my survivor instincts, which have gradually been seized by torpor, and finally gets me back on track.

I don't really understand the utility of the outfit. Who takes the time to don the garb of Jokey Smurf, and why? On the contrary, one would have thought Smurfs to be empty entities, remotely operated and inflated by a *deus ex machina* author, according to the narrative's needs. But how does one put on the essence of the Smurf in his costume? Undoubtedly, I'm getting off track.

I get an idea: Find an exit.

Running towards the opposite end of the corridor, I make out a yellow, or rather straw-coloured, wooden door. Get closer to it, taking a thousand precautions. You never know.

I grab the rough handle of the solid door. Open it to feeble creaks. Glance down the corridor. Nothing. Then thrust my head into the new room. Easily recognize its function. The typical sloping floor, the rows of red velvet seats, the stage curtain, then, between heavy sections of fabric, the white surface of a large screen, nothing poses a problem to my thematic memories. This door opens into a movie theatre.

At the moment, the theatre is plunged into a reassuring semi-darkness. The subdued lighting allows any reader to continue leafing through the pages of their book.

*

Like a newly authorized explorer, I quickly scan the place: no intruders, no suspicious movement, no disturbing signs. I go down the centre aisle, stroking the backs of the seats one by one, like an eccentric prize-winner who's just been called to the stage. I spin around, dance a few steps. Alone in a place that has always given me confidence, I stroll between the seats, sit down in one, play with the spring mechanism.

Interlude.

You could comment that "this is the life," "this is all there is," all we want of the day is to find and permit ourselves this moment of well-earned relaxation, this vague feeling of allowable peace. Our bodies seeking refuge away from the hectic flow of goods and possessions, the automation and digitization of our lifestyles. Me, sovereign for the length of a song, tasting this transcendental freedom that makes me believe I can do anything. Me, well "us," with all the "Is" available today at the market of my potential good fortune.

My feet draw small circles on the theatre's carpeted floor. Head, neck, shoulders in a state of profound passivity allow the events to take over.

*

The theatre has sunken into obscurity, noises have calmly invaded the cinematic enclave, the rolling of film, the rustle of celluloid. Someone is tinkering with the projectionist's tools. A film is about to be screened.

12

A spurt of water. Light made a splash on the screen.

Still no one. I monopolize the theatre. Strange credits slowly roll before my eyes, small branches of text swelling in the flow of a stream, bits of paper floating on a liquid surface.

Imagine a black undulating screen, a calm morning, deep waters collecting and bearing strips of text of various shapes. And without taking into account the spectator's ability to grasp this cinematic machination at first sight. In other words, I'm watching an experimental film.

The overall effect is this:

A foot   *as false as can be*

        a jacket   *over the shoulders*

your eyes

in a virtuoso melody,   *a name*

                                   (*******)

laughing you sing   *delicate chatelaine*

cars and small bells   *montage of a dark lineage*

I would have needed to make these fragments appear one at a time, each traversing the screen alone, diagonally from top to bottom or in an imaginary loop, for you to understand that what I witnessed before me for three minutes proved to be some sort of credits.

Following this short feature, the film began. Its first images: white gravel blemished by wild grasses, a lumbering sun.

Two seats over to my left, a rather thin pretty woman with a soft face sat down. I detected nothing in her behaviour to make me believe she'd spotted me. An attentive spectator.

The composite image with the white gravel continues to unfold onscreen, then a chateau or what looks to be an opulent residence emerges in a languorous tilt-up shot, revealing by the same token the origin of the rough stone surface which traces a long crescent-shaped entrance intended for the vehicles of the mansion's guests. Chateau + crescent-shaped parking + unexpected spectator.

I stretch out.

The anomaly is me.

I wouldn't say that I might have made my theatre companion feel uncomfortable, but rather that my presence leaves her indifferent. It would have made sense for her to be shocked. I don't do anything. I feel her movement and understand that she harbours no aggression towards me. Ignorance alone presides over her coldness.

Stretching, I think it wise to make my presence known. Without actually shouting, which would have been ridiculously tactless, I do what everyone recommends in this kind of situation—a feeble but functional strategy. I start coughing. At first unconvincingly, I fail to assimilate my character's motivations well, then much faster and full of energy.

— Arrr... ohhh... arrr..... huuhuum (clearing of the throat).

She doesn't turn to face me, but addresses me as though I've always been privy to her thoughts, an extra cell on her body in an edifying homeostasis. The young woman breaks the silence.

— It wasn't a wonderful chapter of my life. Well in the end, yes. In retrospect, it was then that it all began to fall apart. You know, with age we understand things better. I did all I could. Gave everything I had. *The Great Gatsby*. I told myself that it would be an excellent TV film. You know the work, of course. The role of Daisy Buchanan, I took up the part that Mia Farrow had so brilliantly played in the previous version with Robert Redford. They told me: "It's a great opportunity." I was still riding on the fame earned from winning the Oscar for best supporting actress in Woody Allen's delirious film. I was definitely the it girl. Had my choice of roles. In 1999. It was in 1999. There, you see the main entrance of this strange aristocratic residence smack in the middle of a working-class neighbourhood in Montreal! Over there, they call this a chateau. We all know it's nothing more than a residence for the well-off. Chateau Dufresne. But Montrealers seem short-changed of grand monuments. They want their chateaus. There is, of course, the huge Olympic Stadium. Oddly, this fails to satisfy them. Anyhow, they asked me to play the role of this amoral girl, Daisy Buchanan, Gatsby's former lover, subsequently unhappily married, who comes back to haunt his life. Loose morals, fickleness, a murder cover-up, an extension of my role as a whore in *Mighty Aphrodite*, only with a nasal twang. They told me: "We'll be shooting in a museum, a heritage house in Montreal." This aspect of working in Montreal pleased me. (Silence.) A French-speaking city. I'd be able to talk with the whole film crew. My French is excellent. Always a pleasure. This metropolis that seems to me like a micro-New York. I never feel like a foreigner there. A profusion of restaurants and culture. I love it. They told me it would be a few days of shooting, some interior scenes in Gatsby's little palace, mahogany wood, fancy mouldings, coffered ceilings, ostentatious luxury.

A million questions come to me, but I hesitate to ask her. I feel it my duty to listen to her, if only because she's finally deigned to notice me or rather, take my presence into account. My curiosity is reluctant to break this audible pact, this tacit understanding that bestows upon her the role of narrating the film we are both watching.

What she says about shooting the film in a pseudo-chateau in Montreal corresponds to the content of the images flashing on the screen. Before this luxurious residence, a large number of technicians, carriers of extension cords, and extras are now bustling about. The tone of her voice, determined, though somewhat melancholic, agrees with the silent film most excellently and seems to complete it. Documentary or news report? The length of the piece will tell.

I am not unduly surprised to see her appear onscreen, a few seconds later, dressed as a young woman of the roaring twenties, a long mother-of-pearl necklace, a headband hat with yellow ribbon. The tone of her voice, at times sentimental, suggests a great deal of nostalgia still in store.

Close-up on her face. She is talking with someone off-camera. Below her chin, a caption in white letters appears.

> Mira Sorvino
> on the making of the TV film
> *The Great Gatsby*

I'm no longer listening to her. Her monologue becomes a tapestry of words, a making-of that loses my interest. More information is given, some of an emotional nature, some more objective.

Besides, who knows what exactly she wants to accomplish by talking to me? It's presumptuous to think myself the intended recipient of this making of the film.

I am alone in a movie theatre flanked by a narrator and her

soothing voice commenting on a report whose soundtrack has been cut.

Then the horde arrives.

13

Out of everything—the ceiling, the screen, the walls, the floor—blue creatures swarm. An infestation, a plague of locusts of biblical proportion, hundreds of Jokey Smurfs surge from all the surfaces. In a few seconds the entire theatre is invaded by this gang of low-lifes. My bewilderment quickly turns to righteous horror. My narrating neighbour disappears, crushed beneath the weight of fifteen laughing revellers.

The loaded packages start exploding here and there, giving off an acrid stench of gunpowder. I knock out at least thirty cartoonish renegades, who have suddenly become terribly passive in their beetlesque carnival. Just as I think the nightmare is about to end, three of these maniacs have the presence of mind to transform me into a target for their presents. Three explosive boxes hit me.

Blackout.

I come to in a busy street in Brussels. My body lies between two horseshoe bike racks planted in the curbstone. A slim man, sporting a ruby sweater and shoulder-length hair, is smoking. He has the lanky, nimble appearance of Brussels people. A limp cigarette hangs between his sticky lips. Spreading his thumb and index finger, as methodically as a sun-baked gecko, he grabs his tube of nicotine, which simultaneously obstructs his face. A simian habit that makes the man look like Siddhartha under his tree.

Some passersby act as a temporary veil between us. An ideal sparseness, managed by a director with a fair eye.

A stagnant cloud of smoke, colonizing his nose and cheeks, gives me the impression that the man is trying to mime a faint conversation. I am delighted by this kinetically stable apparition. Which takes my mind off the chaotic gestures of the blue losers.

I pat and examine myself. I'm in one piece. Well, I'm happy to note all the patching up is still there and the rest of my body perseveres in its state.

Flicking his butt to the ground, the mysterious smoker looks away. An effect of perspective had me thinking he'd been staring at me. I take advantage of this natural transition to stand up, extricate myself from this uncomfortable position. Cigarette man turns on his heels, heads towards the entrance of what looks to be a bookstore.

Upright, I make out the awning more clearly. The word "Pell-Mell" in Cooper Black lettering on a white background is glued to the plastic coating. Craning forward, I discern other incongruous words, "Cat-Sale," on an enormous, recycled, blue sign. The temperature is pleasant, the street empty, the sidewalk hospitable, and the passersby, I must admit, show exemplary courtesy.

Freed at last of all these idiotic hindrances that made a laudable clown out of me, I breathe easy.

I stick out my chest, inhale deeply. Feel I have the right to breathe with gusto and I'm not ashamed. Touch my expanding rib cage, then continue clutching it as it contracts. The ballet of the living, this strange *pas de deux* fills my whole spirit and excites me at the same time. I wouldn't mind having a breathometer. We'd then be able to identify every cycle of inhalation/exhalation. The truth is that we are breathing vehicles. Yet breathing vehicles who have no alternative to recharge, who are only granted the duration of a finite motor, a continuous curve of obsolescence. Objectively speaking, I am midway on the odometer.

A passerby tips his hat at me. Another, in a hijab, holding a doll-like little girl by her right hand and a bag of groceries in the other, notices me and nods her head. I am undeniably part of the world.

The sun is no longer at its zenith. A pleasant twenty-two or twenty-four degrees Celsius appeases all the animals and insects writhing nearby. The planetary homeostasis, culmination of a myriad of complex factors, seems to prevail here. The equilibrium of needs and climate, a true highway for the breathing vehicles, presses on beneath my feet, as it does for my counterparts, a smooth road allowing us to race, chase, skip, walk and perform all other activities essential to comprehending the world.

This highway intended for the breathing vehicles (peaceful, calm, needs satisfied) makes me want to shout out with joy.

I hold back.

Look at me. My disturbed neurons, wooden leg and chocolate arm make me an easy target for sarcasm. On the dashboard of my breathing vehicle, the needle on the emotional odometer is going full tilt. For a moment, I am once again beset by melancholy with its driving acrimony, menacing slope and sullen loathing.

Nevertheless, I manage to get a hold of myself.

The emotional speed limits, demarcated by a team of professionals, make curious guardrails, but bring us some relief nonetheless.

A part of me wants to act better; I listen to it.

Two or three minutes pass. I haven't moved, still standing upright between the bike racks, lost like a tramp from *One Thousand and One Nights* in an international city. Brussels bears me.

I decide to walk on the north side of the street.

A few hundred metres away, on the same side of the street, I find a Delhaize—an outlet of a well-known supermarket chain. I walk in, which sets off a tinkling of bells, and head for the cold section. I'm racked with thirst. I open a fridge, select an orange-flavoured, fizzy drink. Pay and leave.

On the sidewalk, in front of Delhaize, I quench my thirst.

The can emptied, I try to locate a garbage can, notice one farther off, almost near the Stock Exchange.

I walk over.

When the can hits the metal bottom of the small trash can, melancholy overcomes me again, my emotional odometer spinning frantically. The gesture of throwing a crushed can into a commercial container is symbolic; there is nothing I can do about it, it shakes me up.

From the opposite direction, an attractive woman with a fake Vuitton bag, pointy boots and a manga-patterned shirt is blazing a trail of music beats and citrus-scented perfume. Without thinking, I start following her.

Stay four metres behind her, I'm not in a rush, maintaining the appearance of a strolling pedestrian.

Inevitably, my route brings me past the Pell-Mell bookstore from earlier. Contrary to what I'd noticed in the first moments of my brutal landing, the shop window, protecting a phenomenal quantity of books in piles, mounds of yellowed paper, crumbling bindings, paperbacks and hardcovers, is now opaque. My feeling is that a particularly efficient worker selected a thick black paint and quickly accomplished his task of covering the shop window with several coats of the acrylic liquid.

Its long facade is now just a profoundly black wall. From this moment, I forget about my pursuit.

Curious, I scratch the surface with my nails. It's definitely paint.

A sullen-looking man, on unsteady feet, sidesteps me on the sidewalk, mumbles a word of apology rousing me out of my stupor.

My fixedness obstructs the street.

Motorcycles, cars and buses sustain an urban soundtrack on the large boulevard. I inspect my surroundings before retaking my place between two bikes, one turquoise, the other avocado green. An improvised vestibule to reflect in peace.

I face the main entrance. The bookstore's double door is ajar.

Inside, I notice a burst of red.

Feeling timid, I make my chocolate fingers grab the door. The barley sugar digits slide with unsuspected grace. My marzipan nails rap delicately on the inside of the door. I wait a few seconds, ready for anything. Then, reassured, requiring no strength, I effortlessly open the door.

14

Inside the premises, greyness reigns.

The weak light emanating from the back of the room acts like a softener, mellowing the angles of this vast space with no clear function.

Directly ahead in this immense warehouse devoid of books, a slight echo is emanating from a seventies sci-fi film.

As soon as I could identify the ground cover on which I advanced, I bent over to collect a sample.

In my hand: a brochure or prospectus, folded in three sections, with a glossy finish. Blocks of text, Helvetica throughout, some lines in blue, some in red.

The title, left-aligned, of this promotional material tells me nothing.

Universal Bureau of Copyrights

I scan the words of the introductory paragraph.

The Universal Bureau of Copyrights (UniBuC) means to serve any person or company attempting to recover, identify, claim, append, invent, or withdraw a copyright license. UniBuC is under the governance of the rules and regulations of article 1255 of the *Temporary Patents Code* and the International Office of All Existing Property Rights, whether the property be intellectual, speculative, biological, natural, artificial, movables and immovables, even imaginary.

I believe I know what copyright is, but I don't really understand the purpose of this brochure. My thoughts and I are wavering.

Intrigued by these publication chips on the ground, I get down on all fours, sniffing for truffles, dragging my wooden leg along. For some time, I do nothing but gather copies of this prospectus for the Universal Bureau of Copyrights. After handling a good hundred or so of these documents, I give up. My investigation yields nothing. Then, instead of standing up, I tip over on my haunches and sit cross-legged, Indian style.

Relapse into a hypothetical phase.

A black spot on my Neuhaus arm suddenly distracts me from my speculations.

The black mark moves.

An ant.

We kill ants, especially if they take us by surprise. This one didn't stand a chance.

Rummaging through the piles on the ground with two brochures rolled up into stiff tubes, I discover that the floor underneath is covered with only a thin coat of a ligneous material, similar to wood, but which can't be more than seven millimetres thick.

This place looks more and more like an abandoned campsite.

Suddenly, a ray of light disturbs me. The glimmer issues from a vertical crack located approximately sixty metres in front of me. Besides a few ants, a ton of paper scraps covering the floor and a coating of sawdust, nothing prevents me from crossing this distance.

I move closer to the latticed spot.

The air changes. A woodsy aroma gains the upper hand; the dose of olfactory input increases. My nose stays on the scent. At one or two metres away from the hole—a large crooked tear in the black cardboard—the characteristic smell of grasses, leaves, wildflowers and rotting wood assails my nostrils. Using my two hands, I push the long strip of gummy fibres outwards. Straining to enlarge the hole.

A large section of the wall gives way. I fall onto a plateau dotted with grass clumps, stones and shrubs. Regain my balance.

Behind me, an enormous scaffold of wood planks and interminable metal rods forms a gigantic enclosure protecting the structure I've just exited. As far as the eye can see, scenery, scenery and more scenery.

On the earthy plateau, tiny insects, delicate plants, fragile corolla and the waft of moist earth spread every way my eyes turn.

I am completely in nature.

Nearby, as much plain as clumps of shrubs. A profusion of visual stimuli rushes in.

And let's not forget the river down below, before me in plain sight.

15

The river's natural silence captivates me. I attribute feelings to it out of the reflex that protects us against complete solitude, or so I imagine.

Fluids hold secrets.

My thoughts were following their labyrinthine ways when a fearsome storm, a Wagnerian sheet of water, was unleashed on the scenery. A sudden shower, a downpour. Of a climactic violence in its pure state.

Instinct tells me to take cover, but I ignore it. I'd rather run to the river, fling my wooden leg in to test its buoyancy. This profoundly absurd decision doesn't distress me. In uncommon circumstances, why act within the usual limits?

I calculate how long the run will take and decide to head, once my buoyancy test is completed, for an enormous maple, whose branches tilt towards the current, situated about a hundred metres to the north.

A dozen strides is all it takes to reach the river. Water drips into my eyes, penetrates my nostrils, I'm swimming in a vertical pool. My clean clothes have become a veritable coat of mail, protecting me from nothing other than the dread of inexistence. Every ounce of my skin tries to resist the cold with the few resources allotted. Predictably, I'll soon start to shiver. In fact, I'm already shivering. Squatting on the grass, I stretch Encore out and plunge her into the clear juice. The thousands of superfluous ripples the rain makes give me the odd feeling that the liquid is boiling. I'd like to attach a small rope to my leg and make it sail like a miniature sailboat. But the deafening downpour eradicates this possibility. How many of our ideas amount to nothing every day?

It's at this point that I notice a strange reflection a few centimetres below the bubbling soup. A mirror the size of a door is set on a sort of concrete base, a mirror-quay.

Through the liquid puree beating down, I make out the object's outline all the same. The mirror bears no scratches or marks, seems to get regularly polished. A fine line divides it lengthwise in two.

Soaked, I forget for now my project of finding shelter under the maple tree. Being chilled to the bone has made me less irritable. Instinctively, I shake off the river water.

I move over to search out my reflection in the underwater mirror, and remember the power of the saying "it's raining cats and dogs." Try to laugh, but can't quite manage it. Weather-wise, nothing is improving. A lewd wind starts up.

I become acclimatized to the new reality, plunge my flesh-and-bone hand into the current to test the mirror's solidity. My position is wobbly. Fingers confirm the sensation of glass. Dramatically, I knock on the centre of the pane. The water slows down my fist. The wind lashes, doggedly determined to create howling corridors that bend trees over. I feel I don't have much longer to play in the water on the riverbank. Amidst this natural bedlam, only one technical question arises: Is the mirror solid through and through? By kicking the central crack with my wooden leg, I should be able to answer this question.

I grab my fake leg. Stretch my muscles, try to resist the wind, then release an incredible energy to break the reflecting wall. Inadvertently, I slip on some grass. Barely have time to protect my head. Fall with all my weight onto the gleaming surface.

Mouthfuls.

I swallow half a litre.

My scalp is bleeding. My leg has lost a hinge. My back hurts. Improvising, I support myself on Encore by taking the stance of an archer, one knee in the water.

The mirror is as inscrutable as a diamond. Neither cracks nor marks distort it.

A squall. From the other side of the river, I hear a squall.

I should try and get back on the riverbank, though I'm having trouble breathing.

Then the inevitable happens.

The mirror opens from its centre. I fall in.

I struggle. No longer feel the ground, certain I'm dying.

The water continues to roar around me forming a deafening vestibule.

I fall for twenty seconds. Then my face hits a mattress of dead leaves, suffocating me.

16

My nose is bleeding.

I'm in a kind of crypt.

I slowly regain my senses and the ability to formulate thoughts in words and sentences.

The silence feels like a gentle massage.

The Roman Coliseum.

Say it like this to try and convince myself. The Roman Coliseum. It's the first comparison that comes to mind. I see a gigantic hole, encircled by rocky interstices chiselled according to the blueprints of an admirer of the Italian Coliseum. A vast circular structure.

Dumbfounded at the edge of the precipice, my lungs contract. Feel sick, overemotional, before the spectacle of this infernal pit, similar to the one in which Luke Skywalker tumbled down with his one arm missing. My entire body gawks before the grotesque depth of this hole. A great vertical canyon, waterless abyss. Only a space probe could reach the bottom of this sarcastic crater so profoundly does it taunt human smallness. A warm breeze wafts from the bottom, the innermost depths. Our pathetic yearning for individuality gets stuck in our throats before the terrifying, startling, cosmic aspect of this trough built by human hands. No immediate dangers in sight. A quick scan of the horizon gives me an inexplicable soothing sensation. This gargantuan enclosure has its own microclimate.

The time has come to summarize the most remarkable aspects of this subterranean monument. The structure, a colossal shaft, is formed of a single gallery that serpentines along a row of ogives sculpted in the rock face. This produces a series of windows flanked by delicate columns. The ensemble penetrates into the ground as far as the eye can see, in a caricature of perfect perspective drafted in AutoCAD. A vertical grotto of epic proportions. In short, a megalomaniacal project.

Drenched, dirty, injured, limping, and somewhat at loose ends, I turn around.

Modelled on a gentle spiral, the gallery slowly rises on my right to descend in the same manner on my left. The two slopes were drawn to please all manner of walkers. Reduced to a poor walking performance, I nevertheless readjust Encore on her stump, wipe the blood from my head, keep my pants, but abandon all the other dangling tattered clothes without even wringing them out. Bare-chested, I decide to go to the left.

I take off.

Limping, short of breath. Can't continue my descent into the pit beyond three kilometres. On the way, I notice that the rock face is honeycombed with billions of cavities. They cover the gallery's whole interior and, from afar, look like minimalist lace placed over the rock. Inside each one, there is a glass vial the size of a perfume sample, topped with a transparent stopper. The contents intrigue me. I grab a vial, examine it. A meagre grain of rice inside a tube, that's all. I busied myself comparing about thirty of these small containers. Without fail, inside I found a grain of rice of the same size, colour and texture.

Though I am lost, bewildered and in a bad state, only two verbs keep me going: continue, carry on.

17

Chocolate-plated hand propped against the wall of vials, I try to catch my breath. My oppressed lungs cry out. A few other organs also demand a break, much good may it do them.

At three metres from the precipice, I feel vertigo. My eyes turn to the galleries on the other side of the pit.

For the first two kilometres, the setting persisted unchanged. I passed only a reiteration of the same motifs, cavities, vials, Corinthian columns. However, at the start of the third kilometre, the muscles of my healthy leg strained with the effort of the descent, steadfastly stubborn and convinced that to turn back would be unbearably cowardly, absorbing a few beads of sweat tangled in my eyelashes, I made out a physical opening in the rock face across the way. Whether a cavern or room hewn into the rock is still to be confirmed.

About ten minutes later, I reach the spot. The sonic modulation of a human voice welcomes me.

— It's ore.

A man of exotic corpulence addresses me without waiting for me to ask him a question.

He sits behind a counter, caged in a glass box. His soft flesh—pizza dough traversed by veins—gives him a despotic authority. I curb my prejudices.

This large hole in the gallery is a vast office, walls coated with white silicone, somewhat spongy, gleaming, almost electric. The office is more than forty metres deep. The reception area, or what looks like it, runs across the right side of the room. The counter stretches over twelve metres. The receptionist, startled by the presence of a new interlocutor and aroused by the calling of protocol, immediately addressed me with an intellectual weariness.

— It's ore, he said in the same tone.

I tried, at first, to ignore him.

Didn't even bat an eyelid, though he'd repeated his introductory remark twice. Looking for something to give me an air of assurance, I had the presence of mind to finger the texture of the industrial furniture, miming a gesture gleaned from some ads for cleaning products. Gave myself the time to understand the situation of this being. Confined in a huge glass case, reinforced with four metal rings, a slack ocean interrupted by a few islands (eyes, nose, mouth, ears), this man was at the very least eccentric.

The purpose of this place, free of any equipment, screens or wires, didn't appear evident.

Turning my back on the man who put away his syllables after three tries, I suddenly felt forlorn.

Everything leads me to believe that I can retake the gallery towards the centre and pursue my journey with no goal other than discovery and indulgence, not much better than a common thrill-seeker.

When I hear whistling, I come round.

The man doesn't take offence at my lack of civility. His face impassive as a cardboard box, he waits, whistling magnificently. My musical prosthesis, awakened by this occasion of mimicry, starts to hum in chorus with the mysterious clerk. I listen to them respond to each other, blend their timbres, sometimes sing in unison. My detachable leg likes jamming with the stranger.

Bowled over by this melodic mutiny, the only gesture that makes any sense is to unhook my leg and hurl her at the singer's glass prison. I'd started to get fed up with it.

Encore rebounded across the counter.

The two soloists fell silent.

The Leviathan of flesh choked back a sigh of resentment.

Speech surged in my mouth, animated, theatrical, a veritable vital thrust.

— Arrrrrrrrrgggggghhhh.

— It's ore, he repeated.

— But ore of what, and for whom, and how?

A long silence acted like a rampart between us. The true taste of silence took on a thousand variations of tints, attitudes, nanosounds that form the diversity of silent savours. As though a jasmine tea flower slowly unfolded in our respective rib cages, intensifying our presence. A phenomenon I preferred to nip in the bud with a sudden remark.

As I stretch out my arm to collect Encore lying prostrate on the counter, he takes the opportunity to answer me.

— When I say "ore," I'm referring to the grains of rice. You've seen them, I'm sure, in the vials. My more formalist predecessors used the recommended technical term of "copyright nanochips." It's ore, ore of entertainment, ore of ideas. Undoubtedly, you still don't understand what I'm telling you.

— Keep going.

— You are at the Universal Bureau of Copyrights.

— The brochures.

— Our promotional methods are approximate. Themselves dependent on the frequent change of their copyright holders, they reflect only this joyous and beautiful chaos. Nature and culture are no longer separate; they are merged. We have come to a stage of development which entails everything that exists, whether natural or artificial, to be linked to a human right to possession. (Pause.) I know that you read some of our promotional material.

— But how do you know that?

— I'll tell you: everything functions by way of thought. No media will ever again parasitically interfere in the circulation of order. No more intermediary. Thought is now truly recognized as the best interface in existence. Direct implications, direct reactions, direct results. We have managed to develop actual instantaneous communication without a third party. Let me now take a moment to reread you our mission statement:

"The Universal Bureau of Copyrights (UniBuC) means to serve any person or company attempting to recover, identify, claim, append, invent, or withdraw a copyright license. UniBuC is under the governance of the rules and regulations of article 1255 of the *Temporary Patents Code* and the International Office of All Existing Property Rights, whether the property be intellectual, speculative, biological, natural, artificial, movables and immovables, even imaginary."

— Yes, yes.

— I'll confess. I've never met anyone who works for the International Office of Intellectual Property Rights. This organization resembles a secret society. In return, they are the ones who allocated the funds to build the tunnel. For, as you have undoubtedly realized, you are progressing in a kind of pharaonic gas pipeline of the imagination. "Pharaonic gas pipeline" is my expression. In point of fact, the Universal Bureau of Copyrights manages the circulation of the only fuel essential to our mental survival: thought.

— But what about your ore, the grain of rice?

— I'm jumping ahead, I should have first given you some stats. Eighty-six consortia hold all the copyrights in the world, while, every minute, thirteen thousand changes of ownership are recorded, and we open 1,250 new copyright files. To give you an idea of the scale, the tunnel contains approximately $10^{32} \times 10^5$ cavities. In each cavity, you will find a glass microtube containing a grain of rice. To summarize, every word, every material, every object, every letter, every spark of life, every idea, every character, has their copyright. You will understand the magnitude of what I'm saying when I tell you that there is a copyright bill stipulating that all the stones and rocks on earth should have their own copyright from now on. Lucky for us, the original regulation allowed for the granting of copyright to every earthly grain of sand. Ridiculous in terms of storage. The motion was unanimously rejected. But then it made the one for rocks seem more reasonable, which I beg to differ.

— It's Homeric.

— We never get used to it all the same, even though it's our lot. But let me continue: the initial owner who is often the discoverer or inventor of the word, letter, material, object, thing, therefore the precursor owner, we call the Official Copyrighter or, in our bureaucratic jargon, the Off.Cop. This initial ownership, this original copyright of an element of thought, is not eternal. As soon as this first licence expires, whose contract period can range between ten minutes and three years, the temporary owners come in or, if you like, the ones we call the Temporary Copyrighters. Abbreviated, this gives us the Temp.Cop.

— I have a stupid question. Who can own whom or what?

— You're teasing me.

— I'm suddenly afraid.

— We are no longer in an age of complaints and calling into question.

— You haven't answered my question. (*Silence.*) Who owns what, or whom, and what criteria govern the holding of copyright?

— To be honest with you, you yourself are the object of several copyrights. You have no ownership over what constitutes you. It may not be that obvious to you but you will come to understand it. For what it's worth, I myself did not have the luck to own myself at birth, and so you see me here, just as you, overrun by a battalion of Temp.Cop. They are impossible to track down as these copyrights frequently change hands. We get lost in trying to describe ourselves. Without death we would be deprived of self. Moreover, death can only be sold to Special Off.Cop., or Sp.Off.Cop. The Sp.Off. Cop. then orders the death of the unit of copyright according to the terms and conditions that suit them. It's a kind of aggressive yet allowable theft. If they so desire, they can then reactivate as they see fit the grounds for copyright. Therefore, when a Sp.Off.Cop. decides to file a request for a withdrawal of copyright, we no longer have anything to say to our shareholders. Our shareholders—the Temp.Cop. in our jargon—are the initiators of our gestures, behaviours and actions.

— Admittedly, I've always felt dispossessed, especially lately.

— To be in possession of oneself is impossible because several people buy stock options on our destiny right from our conception.

— And my deceived flesh will never know who deceives it, if I understand correctly.

— You are an Arcimboldo painting, a vast amusement site. It's an honour.

I then thought of terms like "epiphany," "advent," "assumption." Decidedly, there is still some religious dust in my trunk. The tone of my interlocutor's voice now shifts. Sweetly, as though taking me into his confidence, he tells me:

— You came here in order to know. (*Pause.*) You came because they wanted you to come. (*Pause.*) You will not leave here without my telling you something they don't wish me to tell you. (*Pause.*) Two consortia, on two continents, are fighting over the networks of Temp.Cop. who...

Before he has a chance to say the right word to suture his sentence, his body swells immoderately in a thousandth of a second to implode in the glass cage and reverberate throughout the place a piercing sound of such unusual nature that none of my references could describe it.

The liquefied human, the sunfish in his cramped fishbowl, has vanished.

The ceiling breaks loose from its gangue.

18

Murky water. All I see is murky water. Sometimes I can breathe, sometimes see, but never with the usual sharpness. Feel like I'm lying on an operating table.

No.

My naked chest is resting on glass. I'm lying on a window-pane, the material is cool, its surface too smooth to be anything other than a pane of glass or some other material cast after melting: metal or mineral.

Someone is tinkering with my one still-viable arm. I don't feel anything. The person doesn't say anything. I don't hear anything. The silence of a bad dream. Keep thinking I'm still alive.

The building is not new, the ceiling, appearing and disappearing in the flux of my senses, looks like one from an old fifteenth-century manor.

*

An elderly, utterly disgraceful, literary tourist is sulking in a corner. She is disgusted with the radical initiative of moustache-man.

With the help of three accomplices—literary tourists joining his rebellion—moustache-man is carrying out a delicate operation.

The guide, it should be noted, has been locked up in the building's public washroom. In the end, he ticked off the rebels who decided to imprison him and carry out this sordid permutation, devised by an evil Doctor Moreau.

— Look here, the ultimate irony, what would it be? Tell me.

Moustache-man insists.

— Agree with me on what it would take to redirect a scene. You had the same information in your hands as me, this home port of Chapter 18. The character, still groggy (fundamental to his person), was supposed to land in the wonderful garden of medicinal plants at the Erasmus House in

Anderlecht. His second arm, wounded, bruised, fractured, was fated for the scrap yard. The original script foresaw that a bunch of medicinal plants were to grow like ivy around the limp limb and restore it.

A young woman, an unobtrusive member of the small group of sidelining literary tourists, dares to speak up.

— What are you doing to the fiction's original ecology? You're nothing but a mediocre patch-it-upper!

— Fine, fine, he says sounding completely bored.

Then a collaborator with protruding eyes intervenes.

— All the books have been carved as needed.

— Excellent. Have you come up with a method for making the joints?

The other more technically-minded stooge retorts.

— I found some twisted iron wire, solid but malleable, that will do for the bones. For the elbow and the mechanics of the digits, I used some very fine ball-bearings.

— Well then, fellows, while the main character is still in the limbo of narrative transition, I ask you to help me here, assist me. We will begin the operation.

*

Gagged behind the store counter, an employee with greying hair and a drooping head is breathing with difficulty. He didn't have time to realize what was happening to him. The narrative's malefactors surprised him from the back. A question of neutralizing everyone not involved in their enterprise of reconstruction. A small bookstore dedicated to Erasmus and his works, this part of the store had lost its principal attraction: twenty copies of *Éloge de la folie*,[3] in the pocket book series from Garnier-Flammarion.

Nulli concedo—I yield to no one—Erasmus's maxim, so often ridiculed it has become a mockery, now serves only to adorn the entrance in wrought iron lettering, screwed into the brick above the door frame.

---

3. *The Praise of Folly*

19

From delirium to delirium, my state doesn't improve.

My own sense of understanding has abdicated. My life is nothing more than a series of ridiculous interruptions in the flow of space-time not worth worrying about. I remain philosophical. If I breathe and all my limbs work, then I still have two or three things to do in this world. It's the first useful thought that occurs to me.

I'm standing on the stairs of the Erasmus House. Some notices and several precise pointers reveal my location.

My two arms are no longer human; my two arms are now only artworks, biogenetic fittings that I have no choice but to bear. It's worth asking if a prosthesis is a handicap or the resolution of a handicap. What is certain is that as we get old, the one thing we wish for our friends is good health. I'm in a good position to conclude that mental and physical health no longer have anything to do with corporeal identity. The important thing today is to maintain the metabolism in a state that keeps us alert, robust, distrustful.

The robustness and mobility of my right arm still surprise me. This thing made of cocoa paste, butter and sugar is a marvel of sophistication. Through means beyond my comprehension, I'm able to make prehensile movements, grasp objects, exert a strong and continuous pressure over any surface that meets my hand.

My strange new arm, made of books of the same size and format (I wouldn't be able to say if it's the same title, but it's conceivable), has been carved out of paper carefully glued by expert hands, trimmed and planed with the meticulousness of cathedral builders. My hand alone consists of several volumes, cut up, trimmed, chiselled, respecting the proportions of my body with phenomenal skill.

Ten minutes is all I need to test and control the motor.

Inspecting the material of my elbow and forearm, I ascertain that it pertains to copies of the same book. The title, appearing only piecemeal on what must have served as the spine of the book, is still discernable by cross-checking: *Éloge de la folie*. A small part of the vast work of the Rotterdam master,

Erasmus. Refined chocolate on my right, work of great learning and knowledge on my left, I can now embrace people with more dignity.

Step by step, I continue to hobble towards the exit. I follow the handrail with the paper hand, which slides along its wooden sister, and I admit that the sensation is not unpleasant. Reaching the ground floor, I stop before a wax bust. In fact, it is a candle that used to look like the bust of Erasmus. The theologian's figure has been reproduced in paraffin. Three-quarters of the head is already damaged, the shoulders will soon follow suit, the chin is starting to melt, as in the centre of what's left of this great humanist's head, a short wick slowly burns at a microscopic rate. The flame, the size of a small pea, eats into the soft material. It is imperceptible, patient, undermining work. This work, by the artist Fabrice Samyn (a cardboard label stuck on the wall tells me), moves me. I get closer to the ravages of heat, stick my bookish finger in the writer's head. A fine coat of the substance amalgamates and dries around my plump forefinger, a diaphanous film proving a deferential exchange of molecules.

In this fifteenth-century building with coffered ceilings and original wood panelling, I am assailed by only one feeling: contemplation. So I use the pretext of this deconstructed statue to spend some moments in silence. I close my eyes.

This spontaneous meditation does me a lot of good. To get lost in silence is to play the game of death, but with Velcro darts. It's relaxing. The room with the decomposing bust adjoins the reception area. While I remain engrossed in this welcoming neutrality, my ever-faithful ears warn me of the presence of an unusual noise. A kind of muffled drumming, as if hitting a sponge affixed to a plank of hardwood. Every house, every building, speaks in its dialect of creaks, one a prolonged sound of cloth being torn, another a grinding twisting noise, others the numerous variations of furtive taps and scratches. All houses stammer or are illiterate and we quickly come to discover their limited vocabulary. However, I don't know the language of the Erasmus House, and confronted with this strange speech, anxiety takes over.

Like a good wannabe theorist, I set out to analyze these noises.

Before long, I hear a long grating moan that roots me to the spot. A sort of yeti-like sound like in *Tintin in Tibet*, an interminable onomatopoeia.

Somewhere in here, there is a man locked up.

With the instinct of a European explorer looking to identify the provenance of a herd of gazelles in an American film about Africa, I crouched down to place my ear against the floorboards. Auricle taut, eye slack, brain on alert, I listened to the lament. After a few seconds of evaluation, I located a spot about twenty metres from me, past the entrance and the shop.

I rose in two stages, necessary given my exotic leg. Without further delay I followed my instinct, and crossed the shop to find a narrow staircase going down to the museum's public washrooms.

Knocked once or twice on the door of the men's washroom.

To properly communicate in these kinds of intensely frightening, febrile moments, we are allowed to make use of reassuring words. These words are few in number: one must know and use them in good taste. I didn't do so badly. We quickly reached a reasonable level of familiarity.

— Are you a friend of Martin Stultitia? Is there still someone in the museum?

— No, no one other than me, I assure you.

The confined man answered me with a long silence. I imagine that the proof quickly germinated in his mind, because he offered me something else besides his muteness.

— Can you get me out of here?

— I'm not too sure how, but this is what I've come to do.

— It's locked. Can you kick down the door? Are you strong?

— I can manage.

Always the same practical idea occurs to me. I unhook my wooden leg. I bet I can demolish this wall with my singing weapon. A problem immediately crops up: staying balanced while swinging a pendulum. The door is two panels feebly held together by thick crossbars across the centre and on the sides. By breaking down the lower part, I'll be able to make a hole through which the man will escape.

*

All this hubbub ends up rousing the shop's sales clerk. He undoubtedly has some kind of plan, since as soon as the hand of the literary tour guide emerges from the jagged hole of the washroom door, the aforementioned man riffles through the bottom of his paper clip dispenser and pulls out a small packet of paper fasteners. He tapes them between his joints with adhesive tape.

*

Encore makes an excellent emergency pole.

Face worn out, shirt torn and hair in tatters, the freed man breathes with gusto, pumping all the air available to him. His cheek to the floor, he doesn't see my face. This gives me time to consider what to say to him.

My act of bravery accomplished, I feel destitute. Glancing at the scratches on the part of his cheek still visible, I gauge his psychological vulnerability and realize that my state won't amuse him. A one-legged man with patched-up limbs—one made of chocolate, the other of Erasmus's *Éloge de la folie*—is not very reassuring. Still have a few seconds to turn around without identifying myself. Like a stork or kangaroo, I shot off on my one leg with a femur to reach the first step of the staircase. Then continued the sport up to the main floor.

Hopping, I reattach Encore and regain my balance. Locate the exit door of the museum. A few metres away. To extricate myself from this place, I must go through the shop again. I start for the hallway, limping quickly along. A two-cent circus mime, a dusty vaudeville. Can't wait to get out.

Just as I'm about to walk through the shop's door, I receive a painful blow to my left eye. I fall over, hit the wall, lose sight of the exit.

20

I'm rolling. Stretched out, tumbling down a gentle slope of weedy lawn that's almost entirely dried out. Cigarette butts, beer caps, bits of tissue, sunflower seeds, McDonald's burger wrappers, I'm sprawled in my own blood on a grubby carpet. Can't see anything, or barely anything, my left eye busted, the blood trailing me, drawing, as though with a Pilot Fineliner, a fine, thin line in the dry zabaglione-coloured grass. Two enamoured young girls stop kissing each other and start staring me down with a hint of fear and a lot of hostility. A black man in his sixties, pitiful, dirty, halts my advance. I bump into him. He's asleep. His slumber is supreme, profound. Miraculously, I don't wake him. He's hot to the touch, damp. The highly potent ammoniac odour he emanates works like smelling salts on me. I pull myself together, exhausted. Flat on my back, I look up at the sky with my one available eye. Before being able to get a clear image of the clouds hanging over me, I have to pass my hand over my eyelashes several times, wipe away some blood, remove a few twigs, and rub off the sandy earth that my tumble has carted along.

The stranger is sleeping on an issue of the journal *Philosophie*. His head is half-resting on an article expounding on freedom in Tolstoy's work. From my viewing angle, I can't read it. I raise myself, lean on my cocoa arm. The citation is slightly curved in, distorted by the weight of the skull of its dozing reader.

Following a few contortions of the eye, I nevertheless manage to decipher the words.

"...we call that which is known to us the law of necessity; that which is unknown, freedom. For history, freedom is only the expression of the unknown residue of what we know of the laws of human life."

Tolstoy reminds me that I am in unknown territory. Which doesn't help me. But what alternative do I have except this circumstantial insight, this resignation that wills me to not be prostrate? I turn back and stare at the horizon. Where there are no answers, there are always, at best, colours and sensations. Inside, I am heartened.

Truly sunk into the abyss, my apathetic companion doesn't move a muscle. I leave him to his dreams.

Bare-chested in a public park (since apparently that is where I am), one doesn't go unnoticed. And even if this is the least unseemly aspect of what defines me, I feel somewhat embarrassed.

Getting up on my feet, I notice three enormous, contemporary metal statues. Three huge totems, hymns to the storefronts of the buildings and edifices surrounding this large green square. I get my bearings. I'm in downtown Montreal, in Émilie-Gamelin Park.

A big, blue bag crammed full of stuff has been left at the foot of one of the vertical geometric statues. Curious, I grab it. Among empty beer cans are some old Iron Maiden, Motörhead and Voivod CDs. At the very bottom, I find a sweater on which someone has vomited. A black pullover.

I let myself borrow this clothing item.

The young lovers have left.

The sun scorches. Yet its violent heat doesn't manage to dry the atmosphere. The sweater retains all its dampness. I look for a fountain to wash the cloth. There isn't one.

The clothing item turns out to be a hoodie, bearing the colours of the band Soulfly. On the front, a zipper vertically divides the cloth, and the word "Soulfly" is written above the breast in shades of brown and ochre. The spray-painted letters imitate ones found on ammunition boxes. Behind them, a kind of motif or tribal mask lords in the centre of a circle drawn in rifle bullets, the cartridge tips pointing outwards.

It's fabulously warlike. It gives off a fetid stink. But I overcome my disgust and put it on. The whole section over the stomach is stained and no one has wrung out the acidic juices.

Near the street, some twenty people are sitting at multicoloured picnic tables or playing giant chess games. I try to thread my way between them, intending to leave the park.

When I reach the first picnic table, a man in his early sixties, entirely covered in tattoos, his blond hair providing a splotch of colour on his shoulders, accosts me.

I keep going, want to be alone.

The man raises his voice.

— Yo, don'cha listen when someone's talkin' ta you? "Rise of the fallen, drink from the fountain of your poisoned dream," fuckin' great.

I turn on my heels, ready to bolt. Two steps away from me, he changes his tone.

He's got a jean jacket, a Megadeth T-shirt and a plain sweater with a zipper.

— Hey man, wait a sec, wait. Do ya feel like exchanging your gross Soulfly hoodie for my super-clean one?

This groupie has come at just the right time. I feel like this whole saga of sartorial dignity will soon get settled. I'm about to formulate a kind remark and accept his deal when David Foster Wallace, disguised as a cop, intervenes.

— Everything all right here?

The Soulfly fan waves his hands, brushes the air in circles, as if he wants to polish the emptiness around him. He slowly turns back. The writer-patroller takes the opportunity to grab me by the arm.

The sun plummets.

21

I'm suffocating, breathing a warm liquid.

A man in a red turtleneck and work overalls brushes against my knees, heads straight for a wall at the foot of which my head swims. I hear his fly open. A thick warm stream shoots out, taking on the shape of a slender downward curve. The liquid is not projected at a speed to cause a splashing noise. The discharge only produces a flowing sound. The steaming water trickles down the brick wall, completing its course in a shallow basin overlaid with beige ceramic tiles. The man passes a hand through his greasy hair while attending to the urination's flow with the other.

He zips up his fly and passes me again without noticing my presence.

There is a crowd of men moving about on this street. Their actions are synchronous, they all walk on the left side of the road, at times pretending not to notice the contents of the windows. Then, one or two storefronts further on, they try to clumsily hypnotize someone. Their game fascinates me.

Now seated on the ground, hands clasped by reflex, I look like a man deeply engrossed in devotion. But I'm just resting. My appearance indicates *otium*, the sport of contemplation, idleness understood as a spiritual discipline, but my body is entirely steeped in calculations of *negotium*, from the sphere of negotiation, the throes of competition, the implementation of this inconsolable forging ahead that we call "business." I seem to be on vacation, but think only of finding a way out. Fleeing with the look of triumph, fleeing with the haughtiness of one who seems to have conquered chance. Today, there is no longer any difference between these two states. *Otium* and *negotium* get mixed up.

The structure of the strange ritual I observed a few minutes ago appears to remain undisturbed. My materialization should have alarmed a few curious onlookers, bothered the passersby, but I sense no change in their attitude.

A prodigious silence, programmed, staged by engineers, rules. Only the windows prompt a few conventional reactions, summed up in a few words: inspection, judgment, indifference or hypnosis.

I head towards the first storefront on my left.

I stand before it.

In the window on a wooden stool, wearing a baby-doll dress and extravagant makeup, sits the comic strip heroine Bécassine, offering her ample breasts and rustic ass. In the middle ground, a curtain of multicoloured tulle blocks the view of another room, presumably the one with the bed.

Ignoring my presence, an extremely short gentleman with badly fit glasses rings the doorbell nearby. Bécassine moves from her enticing pose and stands, while the lecherous old man gives some money to a madam who welcomes him into the shop. They draw the tawdry curtain of tulle.

Any minute now, I expect to run into Jokey Smurf in this carnivalesque decor. Keep my guard up.

As I continue to walk past the businesses, I alternately see Natasha having to manage the clientele bustling around her; Mafalda trying to tame her stool; Yoko Tsuno, of an ethereal beauty, effortlessly selecting her buyers; then, a dozen manga characters, Megumi, Nana, Hina, Cindy, Satie, characters from *Seraphic Feather*, Karin from *Chibi Vampire*, Masakazu Katsura's Video Girl, Cha Young-mi from *Daddy Long Legs*. I don't know anything about these adolescent personifications, hewn by a Modigliani retrained in whiteness, but I see the commotion that the appearance of these naiads causes in common sensibility. I'm able to identify them thanks to stickers at the base of the large windows, imitating photo captions in magazines.

The more I progress on this street, the more the livestock seems to increase. Also, I'm forced to hide from a Smurf with a present, a gleaner stroking with asinine delight the transparent wall preventing him from fondling Tsukushi Makino, a fantasy hackneyed from the manga *Hana Yori Dango* about a young Japanese student in a neat and tidy uniform. Right then, two big Americans with smiles on their lips come out from backstage of Tsukushi's show. I want to slip away. A group of febrile North Africans offer a terrific shield for concealing me from the melancholic Smurf. I advance behind my screen of merrymakers when I see the young Makino return to test-market her attributes, ignoring with a clinical coldness the blue beggar's presence, who jerks off his regret on the window blocking all access to his beauty.

Near the entrance to the Brussels-North railway station, I notice an empty booth, marked with the label "Vicky and Jenny" from the *Bellybuttons* series. Whether they're absent or occupied I'll never know, because I decide to pursue my exploration inside the railway station. Hundreds of people mill about the large hall with multiple stairwells. Worry seizes me when I recognize these humans' excessive pallor, their skin almost entirely washed-out, including that of all their bodily extremities. I feel I'm standing before a new representation of the body rather than my memory of human beings.

I slip.

22

— Judith and Holofernes...

His eye materializes. It is open, wrinkled. He blinks. Nestorius-Didi doesn't rush things and recognizes the importance of all classifications, those we teach in school and those we guess, by living, to be connected to human relationships, proportional to what these contacts imply.

Before this character's wide-open eyes, the central path of the Cinquantenaire Park in Brussels traces its ostentatious perspective to culminate in the three stone arches designed by architect Charles Girault. This monumental work is surmounted by a grandiose bronze sculpture, "a quadriga," representing four galloping horses pulling the chariot of the Duke of Brabant (more or less the city founder).

The obsessive symmetry of the site recalls the plans of the Fascist monuments commissioned by Mussolini to show off

Rome and promote the dehumanizing ideals of vivacity, energy and radicalism championed by the Blackshirts regime.

A silence, compressed by the military sumptuousness of the place, spreads from the Avenue de la Renaissance to the Avenue des Nerviens.

Our man, advanced past retirement age, sports a white bow tie under a starched collar of the same tone, a black and yellow striped suit and shined old-fashioned shoes. His legs, swathed in black, impeccably pleated pants, keep him upright. A strip of hair barely four centimetres wide crowns his head at ear level. The rest of his skull is bald.

Having just exited the Schuman subway entrance a few minutes ago, the servant enters Cinquantenaire Park and, notwithstanding a brief hesitation, chooses a direction he seems to recognize.

An observer seated on a nearby bench would have noted, in the choreography of the gentleman's stroll, a slight pause taken on the central path, followed by a rolling gait towards the side of the Avenue de la Renaissance. The entire, brief, intimate dance lasted no more than a few seconds.

The man in livery took a diagonal path leading to the main

path lined with sycamores and silver maples. Old wood greened by lichen, high branches cast in the air in the style of the imploring hands in the famous *Guernica* painting.

Stray readers, dog-walkers, pairs of friends and German tourists, wan, resolutely dull, lacking all colour that produces joy yet not deathly pale, are scattered throughout the area, doing all they can to go unnoticed. They succeed.

Picking up the pace yet not running, the man devoid of hair on the top of his skull gives the impression that he's mimicking autumn with his face of falling leaves.

Some twenty metres away, the main character, sprawled unconscious on a bench, his abnormally ashen left arm dragging on the ground, is allowing three crows of an extremely pure Pantone metallic black to peck away at him. One of the winged creatures attacks his right eye—an old potbellied Parisian dipping a bread finger in his boiled morning egg.

On one side, the man walking, on the other, the main character, hardly moving, lying bare-chested on a bench, head resting on a black sweatshirt. Shot, reverse-angle shot. The walker picks up his step.

With a strong kick and a few sweeps of his arm, Nestorius-

Didi drives away the birds. The leanest crow seems aggressive as it opens its curiously pixelated beak. The other diners, wildly beating the air, reveal tiny medallions etched with the word "Tirby" beneath their wing feathers.

Nestorius-Didi can't recover. He frets.

His heart begins to pump much more blood per second. A slight headache overcomes him.

— Judith and Holofernes... Artemisia.

Sniffing the air around the sleeping man's head, Nestorius-Didi notes the presence of a slight whiff of alcohol. Curious, he looks for the odour's origin, shoves the anesthetized man to find a bottle of Loch Lomond Single Malt Scotch Whisky under the bench. He turns his back on the blind man, meticulously unscrews the bottle and takes a good swig to calm his nerves. He remains stock-still while the expected effect permeates his body. He downs another shot of the cask-aged liquid while examining the sleeping man's face.

Out of respect for the drunkard (he uses this word in his mind, although at most 20 ml of scotch was missing from the bottle when he grabbed it), he returns the bottle to the exact spot he found it.

*

Nestorius-Didi is now in the Napoleonic Wars Room of the Royal Museum of the Armed Forces and Military History, which takes up the northern section of Cinquantenaire Park.

He's just found what he was looking for in a glass case. He removes his jacket and lays it against the glass. Holding the jacket in place with his left hand, he punches the obstacle with the other, intending to break it. The glass bursts. His hand, sore but not wounded, reaches towards his desire. A security guard in uniform mechanically does his rounds, taps his kepi, walks around the thief, even greets him by taking off his cap, and passes by the smashed case, clearing his soles of any sharp tips and glass shards.

The ordinary tourists reading the wall texts and labels, museum's panels and displays, are not in the least bit alarmed to see a butler gasping for air, visibly stunned, dragging a sheathed Mameluke sabre swiped from the collection.

This curved weapon, a French transplant of the original Egyptian model, was first used by the new regiment of Mamluk soldiers in the Battle of Austerlitz. A classic scimitar-like sword, this piece figures in a wonderful Girard painting celebrating the great Napoleonic victory of 1805.

— Artemisia...

A clock and its cuckoo. This is what the figure of Nestorius-Didi might have resembled upon exiting the museum. Sabre brandished at chest level, he flings open the door, leaves with such a lack of civility, that they crash into the outside wall.

Comet or mad firebrand, our servant is no longer a master of his own mind.

This new sabre-donning man no longer lives in a world of complicity or of the good word; he now pursues only a strange desire for accomplishment expressed through the resoluteness of his actions.

A few minutes prior, we could have still laughed at his clumsiness, his embarrassing attention, his mild mischievousness, but now only a vague timorous murmur escapes the closed lips of the passersby.

We hesitate.

To move is to become the same. To not be the same is to age.

In our inner depths, the ancient ovens of common wisdom still heat, fed by the tepid thoughts that comfort us.

Nestorius-Didi returns to the bench and the bottle of scotch with a determined step.

Trampling on the walkway's gravel, his shoes make the slight crackling sound of a needle skipping on a record.

Still prone, his head on a sweatshirt, the blind man with the wooden leg doesn't jump when a hand suddenly grabs his hair.

Dissatisfied with his staging, Nestorius-Didi first pulls the man's slumped body towards him, so that his neck disengages from the cushiony sweatshirt and conveniently juts out from the end of the bench. He then strikes a pose with his weapon.

The false arms of the unfortunate creature, warned too late of imminent danger, stiffen and wave in all directions. A strike of the sabre finishes off, at elbow level, the all-too-insistent chocolate prosthesis. The paper arm hits the ground, not managing to free the sabre from the beleaguered neck. Nestorius-Didi applies himself heart and soul to his decapitation project.

An old, patched-up, antiquated sculpture defending itself against the inevitable.

Nothing more. This is what a basset hound owner thinks at the same moment, witnessing the crime. We could have said an ordinary *Venus de Milo* victim of an attack.

Following a few patient attempts, the head dies, the liquids slip out.

*

At the end of this summer afternoon, in Cinquantenaire Park, the hole is there, as it is everywhere, and life goes on.

23

"--我们要你把白求恩的脑袋适应在人物身上...

涅斯迪迪返回到舒曼地铁站，在蒙特利尔康考迪亚地铁站下车, 出站.

他像受遥控一样移动. 在他的最后一个级的身体里, 一切运行正常. 他快速地走了几米来到白求恩广场. 一家代表加拿大医生白求恩的大型，白色雕像在广场中间立着. 他毫不踌躇地攀登雕像, 到半身像并开始动手把雕像的颈部锯下来."

(Etc.)

Notes

This novel was written in several locations. The first pages of the book saw the light of day in Brussels, in the Passa-Porta studio, as part of a writer residency sponsored by the Conseil des arts et des lettres du Québec, in January and February 2009. Another section was written during a short retreat at Horeb Saint-Jacques, at the beginning of June 2010. The rest of the novel was imagined in my former Montreal apartment on Sherbrooke Street, then in my girlfriend's soothing house in Saint-Ligouri, during the spring and fall of 2010 and the winter of 2011.

Thank you to my English translator Oana Avasilichioaei for the elegance and poetical vision with which she approached the translation of this book, and to my Toronto publishers Hazel and Jay for their magnificent enthusiasm!

Lastly, I would like to thank the swiftness and generosity of translator Robin Dumont, who was gracious enough to translate the novel's last chapter into Mandarin, reproduced below in its original version:

"— We'd like you to fit Bethune's head on the character's body.

Nestorius-Didi returns to the Schuman subway station, then comes out of the Guy-Concordia subway station in Montreal.

He is operated by remote control. Once he reaches the upper level of the station, his body functions perfectly. He walks a few metres and quickly comes onto Norman Bethune Square. A large white statue of the Canadian doctor reigns in the centre of the square. Without a second thought, he climbs onto it, reaches the monument's head, and begins to saw with conviction the statue's neck."

(Etc.)

*

Trans.

A special thank you to Gregoire Pam Dick, the translation's first reader, for her sharp eye and excellent suggestions, and to the BookThug team, Jay and Hazel Millar and Malcolm Sutton, for their efforts.

About the Author

BERTRAND LAVERDURE is an award-winning poet, novelist, literary performer and blogger. His poetry publications include *Rires* (2004) and *Sept et demi* (2007). He has written four well-received novels, *Gomme de xanthane* (2006), *Lectodôme* (2008), *J'invente la piscine* (2010), *Bureau universel des copyrights* (2011). *Lettres crues*, a book of literary correspondence with Quebecois author Pierre Samson, was published in the fall of 2012. Most recently, he published a YA poetry collection, *Cascadeuse* (2013). Awards include the Joseph S. Stauffer Prize from the Canada Council for the Arts (1999), and the Rina-Lasnier Award for Poetry for *Les forêts* (2003). *Les forêts* was also nominated for the Emile-Nelligan Award for Poetry (2000), while *Audioguide* was nominated for the Grand Prix du Festival International de Poésie de Trois-Rivières (2003), and *Lectodôme* for the Grand Prix littéraire Archambault (2009). Find Laverdure on his blog, http://technicien-coffeur.blogspot.ca/, follow him on Twitter @lectodome, or connect with him on Facebook https://www.facebook.com/bertrand.laverdure.

About the Translator

OANA AVASILICHIOAEI's previous translations include *Wigrum* by Quebecois writer Daniel Canty (2013), *The Islands* by Quebecoise poet Louise Cotnoir (2011), and *Occupational Sickness* by Romanian poet Nichita Stănescu (2006). In 2013, she edited a feature on Quebec French writing in translation for *Aufgabe* (New York). She has also played in the bounds of translation and creation in poetic collaboration with Erín Moure, *Expeditions of a Chimæra* (2009). Her most recent poetry collection is *We, Beasts* (2012; winner of the QWF's A.M. Klein Prize for Poetry), and her audio work can be found on Pennsound. She lives in Montreal. Learn more about Avasilichioaei at www.oanalab.com.

Colophon

Manufactured as the First English Edition of *Universal Bureau of Copyrights* in the fall of 2014 by BookThug.

Distributed in Canada by the Literary Press Group: www.lpg.ca

Distributed in the USA by Small Press Distribution: www.spdbooks.org

Shop online at www.bookthug.ca

BOOK
PRODUCTION
WAR ECONOMY
STANDARD

Type + design by Jay MillAr
Copy edited by Ruth Zuchter